CAIN

THE WAITE FAMILY
BOOK *1*

KATHI S. BARTON

This is a work of fiction. Names, characters, places, and incidents are products of the author's imagination or are used factiously and are not to be construed as real. Any resemblance to actual events, locations, organizations, or person, living or dead, is entirely coincidental.

World Castle Publishing, LLC
Pensacola, Florida

Copyright © by Kathi S Barton 2012
ISBN: 9781938243165
Second Edition World Castle Publishing LLC April 15, 2012
http://www.worldcastlepublishing.com

License Notes

Cover: Karen Fuller
Editor: Brieanna Robertson

~*CHAPTER ONE*~

Cain watched the woman across from him beneath his lashes. He had just laid his head back and closed his eyes when she walked in and sat down. He hadn't really paid any attention to the girl until the nurse told him not an hour ago that his mother's surgery was about to begin.

"The doctor said he'd be another hour, Julie. He wants to know if you'll see another doctor or can you come back tomorrow."

Shifting so that he had a better view, but not yet opening his eyes, Cain listened to what was going on. He was slightly uncomfortable when the girl, Julie, stared at him for so long, but she moved her gaze to the next person before she looked down again.

"If you'll just give me Rodney's medications, I'll go now. It's not all that bad. I've kept the cut clean."

"Julie, please let another doctor see it. I can tell you hurt. I know you won't come back until Rodney needs his medications again. What if it's too late by then?"

Julie didn't say anything. After a minute, the nurse patted the girl's hands that were tight in her lap and got up.

Cain opened his eyes and looked around the room. He was trying to appear as though he'd just awakened. He stood and stretched as he moved to the open doorway and out into the hall. The nurse was going toward the main desk. He followed her.

"Is there something I can help you with, Dr. Waite? If it's food, I'm afraid the cafeteria only serves cold sandwiches this time of morning."

Cain almost shuddered. The thought of eating hospital food again nearly made him ill. He swore that once he had taken the state exams and become a doctor, he'd never eat it again.

"Thanks, but no. I was wondering about the girl, the one in the waiting room just now. Do you know why she needed a physician?"

The nurse flushed. "She is a very private person, sir. Julie said she'd been hurt and wanted someone to stitch it up for her. And as we all know, for her to ask for help means she must really need it." While that didn't answer his question, it did tell him that Julie was a regular here.

"And Rodney? Her husband, I'm assuming?" He didn't know why he cared, but he did. He was surprised by her answer.

"No, sir, Rodney is my brother. He lives on the streets, as does Julie. Hard times, you know. But neither of them will take what they consider handouts. If there's nothing else, I've work to do."

Cain hadn't meant to hurt her feelings. He'd only been asking, and to be honest, he was bored. He was here because his mother had requested he be. He didn't know why. They barely spoke to one another and had lived on different ends of the United States for years. But she had needed to have a cyst removed from her breast and she'd come to Ohio to have it done. He'd taken the offer from his partners from the private practice he'd been at in Maine some time ago and was just getting around to settling in Ohio when she called. He hadn't even had time to purchase a house yet, much less set up a new practice.

"I'm sorry, Molly, I'm a little stressed. I was merely asking because I thought I'd help her. Damon Grant can vouch for me. We've been friends for longer than I can remember. He used to have the hots for one of my relatives a while back."

"Dr. Grant is married now. He has a lovely son and daughter too. I'll just give him a call and then see if Julie will let you treat her."

Cain went back to the waiting room to see if he could convince the girl to let him help her. It became a moot point when he found her crumbled on the floor in a pool of blood.

~~~

Julie woke slowly. The dream she was having was just too wonderful to let go of so soon. She was warm, something she only felt in the summer, and she felt like she was sleeping on a cloud. Of course, sleeping on the hard ground for so long, sleeping on even a thin pad would feel like a cloud. When she rolled over, she felt the first bit of fear. Her leg wouldn't move.

"It's been immobilized so you wouldn't pull out the stitches in your belly. I had to put in fourteen and the skin there moves so easily, I didn't want you to have to be put under again to repair it. Do you need anything?"

Julie looked over at the man who spoke. It took her several seconds to get him to come into focus then another two to remember where she'd seen him. He was the guy from the waiting room.

"Clothes? I'd like my clothes, please." She noticed the IV in her hand and thought about taking it out. But she didn't have much energy right now and was conserving her movements so she could leave.

"I'm afraid I had to cut your pants from you. Your shirt didn't fare much better. I'm not sure what the nurses did with them. I would imagine that they were thrown out."

Julie doubted it. The staff here knew who she was and also knew she'd pitch a bitch fit if they ever did that again. When she'd been brought in several months ago, they'd cut her clothes then too. Julie pulled the nurse call button and ignored the man sitting in the chair next to the bed.

"Yes, Dr. Waite. What can I do for you this fine evening?"

Julie cocked a brow at the grinning man. "It's Julie. I'd like my stuff please. I also need one of those 'get out of jail free' papers too. I'm ready to check out."

"Yes. All right." The nurse's tone was decidedly less breathy and much more professional. Julie smiled as she leaned back on the pillows.

The door opening had her look up. The person standing there made her groan. Margaret Parker. Julie laid back and closed her eyes quickly.

"Don't you dare pretend you're sleeping, young lady. We had a deal. You said if you got hurt again, you'd come stay with me. Well? Are you ready to get off the streets now?"

Julie glanced at the man who had stood when Mrs. Parker came into the room. Then she looked back at the older woman. "Our deal was if I got beat up again. I didn't. So go away. I'm just waiting on my stuff then I'm out of here." Julie nearly laughed out loud when Mrs. Parker stomped her foot. The man did laugh and was rewarded for it by Margaret turning on him.

"Cain Waite, you are not too big for me to spank again. Instead of laughing at a poor old woman, you should be using your considerable charm on that one." Julie turned to see who was behind her when Margaret pointed at her. "I know you have some. I also know you charmed Becky Shaffer out of her bra when you were nothing but fifteen years old."

The man didn't look to Julie like he needed to do more than look at a woman and she'd gladly peel out of whatever he wanted her to. Eyes to die for, as her mother used to say. Dark green eyes with long lashes over his tanned skin. His light blond hair looked like it had been kissed by the sun a great deal. It was so curly she'd bet he had to brush it several times a day just to keep it in some sort of order. He towered over Mrs. Parker, who Julie knew to be about five-foot-five. Julie knew that he would be at least six or more inches than her own five-foot-nine. He was dressed in a dark polo shirt with the top two buttons opened, and just enough hair peeked out to let her knew he was deliciously furred beneath his clothes. His chest looked strong and she caught herself wondering if he was married when she heard him clear his throat.

Somehow, Julie knew he was aware of her every thought when her eyes slammed to his. She didn't have to know that her cheeks were hot to the touch. She could actually feel her skin burn with embarrassment. She felt stupid and when she felt that way, her temper got the better of her.

"I doubt he could charm me if he had all the time in the world. I don't charm. Better luck next time, Mrs. Parker. I'm—"

"Not going anywhere. Hello, Julie. You and I have a deal, remember? You said that the next time there was blood spilled, I get what I want. And I have a waiting room that says I win," Damon Grant said as he stalked to her bedside. "Now, I know Cain to be a great doctor, but just so you can verify the spilled blood part, let's have a look, shall we?"

Julie held tight to the sheet and when he pried her fingers back one at a time, she knew she couldn't escape. "I hate you," she said to him. Damon laughed. Then when he motioned for the other man to come forward, she tried to fight the sheet back into place again.

"I assure you, Julie, this is for your own good. Let go of the sheet and let us examine this. Come on, be a good girl."

Julie knew she was trapped. The blood part was why she'd been trying to see the other doctor and not Damon. Ben Samuels wasn't as nice or as friendly, but he wasn't Damon Grant.

"He goes. He wasn't part of the deal. He goes outside with your mom or I...or I start screaming." Both men stared at her. "You know I will, Dr. Grant. You've tested me before." When no one moved, Julie took in a deep breath to do just as she'd threatened. Dr. Waite stepped back. He glared at her for so long that she was sure he was going to call her bluff. Then before she could relent, he turned on his heel and left the room, Mrs. Parker on his arm.

~CHAPTER TWO~

Cain paced the hallway. Damned girl, what did she think he was going to do? Pounce on her? Beat her butt? He'd put the damned stitches in her, for the love of Christ.

Cain stopped his pacing when he noticed the nurses eyeing him strangely. Running his fingers through his hair for what seemed like the hundredth time, he looked over at Mrs. Parker.

"Don't you glare at me, young man. I don't know why she threw you out. I do know that she's as stubborn as I've ever seen a woman and most of the time I want to shake some sense into her. But that's about all I know."

"Do you know why she's homeless?" At her surprised look, he continued. "She was here for one of the nurse's brothers. Meds, I think."

"That would be Rodney. Yes, Julie has been caring for him for a couple of years now. She comes in and gets his diabetic and mental health medications for the week. He's healthier than he's been for years. Did she tell you how she got hurt this time?"

Cain looked at the closed door. Other than asking for her clothes, she'd not said anything to him. "No, ma'am, she didn't. Will Damon be able to find out?"

Before she could answer, Damon stepped through Julie's door and into the hall. The look on his face showed he wasn't any happier with Julie than Cain was.

Damon stood there taking several deep breaths before he spoke. Then it was to ask them to wait here, he needed to see the nurse in charge. Cain sat down next to Mrs. Parker.

Cain had known the Grants since he was in middle school. His house, when growing up, had been just down the street from what was now the Parker house. The Grant boys were all grown then, but Cain still hung around them. Theirs was what he'd always wanted in a family. When Cain had gotten hurt at a high school football game and broke his ankle, Damon had taken him to the hospital. His parents hadn't gone to the game—his mother had been too drunk and his father had been off with one of his other women; in other words, they'd been too busy to be there.

Mrs. Parker had gone to the house to let them know he'd been hurt and had brought his five younger sisters to her house. Mrs. Parker had never said another word, but soon after, someone from Children's Services had come and taken them all away. As soon as Cain could, he'd made sure his sisters were with him.

Cain's father had gone to prison in Cain's first year of med school and had just recently been released. The senior Waite, Roscoe, had been trying to contact Cain since the day he got out over four weeks ago.

Cain stood when Damon returned. Mrs. Parker told both men she was going home. Each kissed the elderly lady's cheek and told her goodbye before Damon spoke.

"They gave me an office here. Come on, let's go there to talk. I've not set it up yet, but I know the furniture has been delivered."

They were sitting down when Damon's phone rang. Cain sat back and looked around the spacious office. There were boxes of stuff everywhere. He could see that someone had hung a few pictures and a few of Damon's certificates. The room smelled clean with the slight undertone of cigar smoke. Since Cain knew that Damon didn't smoke, he thought it belonged to his predecessor.

"That was Charlotte. She said to tell you that you're coming to the house for dinner tonight. I wouldn't argue with her. She's having major empty nest syndrome and cries about everything."

Cain smiled. "So when did your daughter move out? It had to have been recently."

"Three weeks ago. I thought it would be hard on her when Connor moved out, but it's nothing compared to this." Damon sat up, giving Cain what he had always called his "I'm gonna come down on you cause I love you" look. "Thanks for seeing Julie. If you hadn't volunteered, Molly wouldn't have called me. Julie is...I'm not even sure if that's her real name. But she's pretty special to my mom and me. All of us really."

Cain was a little startled by the tears in Damon's eyes, but didn't comment on them. Cain looked away again to give Damon a minute to get himself together. When Damon cleared his throat, Cain looked back.

"I'm sorry. Whenever I think...she saved Connor's life about three years ago. He'd been out with a bunch of his friends and they'd been drinking. Connor...the accident killed three of the kids. Connor's only alive because Julie pulled him to safety just before the car blew. She stayed with him until help came. I was there when the medics told her that he was too far gone to save. My God, you should have seen her." Damon smiled at the memory. "She told them she was going to beat the shit out of him if he stopped trying. When he looked like he was going to hit her, she punched him square in the nose and did CPR herself until someone else stepped in with a defib."

Cain's estimation of the girl went up a few more notches. "Do you know what happened tonight? Why she needed medical attention?"

"No. The damned girl. Like I said, I'm not even sure what her name is. Whenever she brings one of the indigents in, they call her by something different. Rodney calls her Julie, as does Molly. I have never heard her last name. And wouldn't even be sure if that was it or not. She is...I've never met a more private person in my life."

Cain thought about Molly talking to Julie. Molly seemed to be very familiar with her and he wondered if the nurse knew more than she was letting on.

"Now what happens to her? You two have a deal, but how long do you think you'll be able to keep her here with just that? She doesn't strike me as a cooperative person."

Damon sat back in his chair before answering. For reasons he wasn't sure of, Cain just knew he wasn't going to like what Damon was going to say. He started to tell him to forget he asked when Damon dropped the bombshell.

"Julie doesn't like it, but I told her you were her doctor. I know this Chief of Surgeon gig is only until they find someone to replace Gabe, but I was enjoying my part-time status as a doctor and I don't want to have to change things around now. I just don't have the time for someone as stubborn as Julie right now."

Nope, Cain thought, *not at all*. Before he could protest, Damon went on.

"You can't be all that busy right now. I know you just moved back and all. And one slip of a girl won't take up too much of your time. Not really. You don't mind helping out an old friend, do you?"

Cain threw back his head and laughed. Damon had just neatly boxed him in. Not that Cain minded all that much, but Damon had him right where he wanted him. "I don't have privileges here yet. My application is still awaiting final—"

Damon picked up his phone and just like that, Cain could now practice at Ohio State University Hospital.

"Do you happen to know of a house too, Oh Mighty One? I'm tired of living in a hotel. I want something with several bedrooms for when the girls come to visit. And anyone wanting to take on a partner with option to buy in?"

"Partnership? Hum, let me think on that one. Devin's house is empty right now. Well, it's furnished, but he isn't living there. I think he may sell it to you cheap. It has six bedrooms and a nice two bedroom cottage out back. With him and Ronnie in Washington so much since he got into politics, they aren't here as much as they once were. I'll talk to him tomorrow. Come on, let's get you settled in with Julie, then we'll go back to my house."

Cain smiled. He had a patient, a house, and a job. Not bad for three hours work. He went by to check on his mother again and was relieved she was still asleep. Damon and he entered Julie's room five minutes later.

~~~

Julie was playing with her food when the men walked in. She'd always thought Damon was handsome, but the younger man, Cain Waite, was beautiful. She was still embarrassed at him catching her staring at him. His grin told her that he hadn't forgotten either.

"You're supposed to eat it not roll it around on your plate. I told you that you needed to clean plate everything they brought you," Damon said when she shoved the tray away.

"Fine. You tell me what sort of food this is supposed to represent and I'll gladly eat it. Or drink it in this case. How do you expect someone to get better when you feed them water? It even smells rank. I thought you said you were leaving. Is it too much to hope you're finally going to leave me alone?"

"I came to give you a good night kiss and to make sure you remember what I said. You do remember, don't you, Alice?"

Julie noticed the confused look on Dr. Waite's face. "He thinks he'll be able to guess what my name is like this. You know, say a name and see if I react to it. What he doesn't realize is that I don't care if he ever guesses. So no matter what he guesses, he's shit out of luck," Julie explained.

"Behave, Julie, or I'll tell Becky to be your nurse tonight."

Julie shut up. She hated Becky. The girl didn't have a compassionate bone in her body and she hated Julie as much as Julie did her. She grabbed the sheet when Damon was about to pull it back from her. But let go when he raised a brow at her. Closing her eyes, she leaned back hard into the pillows.

The wound was a long slice across her belly. She knew it was bad. She'd been trying to take care of it on her own for two days. Julie couldn't even stitch it on her own; her breasts kept getting in the way.

Moon, Julie wasn't sure what his real name was, had sliced her open when she'd come across him sleeping in the rain one night. Someone had peed in his box and when Julie had touched his shoulder to wake him, he'd come at her with the knife, raking it across her belly in a heartbeat.

It was deep and it had bled like an artery had been cut. For a few minutes after it had happened, she was sure Moon had eviscerated her, spilling her guts out on the cold, wet ground. Julie had tried taping it closed, but she had started to pass out from blood loss and had gone to the hospital. She'd had to pick up Rodney's meds anyway.

"Julie, look at me, please? I'd like to judge how much pain you're in when I touch around the stitches."

"It fucking hurts. I don't think you looking at my face is going to make a spit of difference," she told Dr. Waite.

"Julie...I'm serious. You want me to call Becky to come in here and sit with you?" Julie glared at Damon. With a low "prick," she looked at Dr. Waite.

Cain was laughing. She wasn't sure if it was at her or Damon, but figured it was at her. When he pressed a little too hard on her sore belly, she had to bite her lip to keep from cussing at him. As it was, she called him plenty in her mind. His apology had her look at him again.

"When can I leave?" she asked as he finished up. "He said three days." Julie jabbed her finger in the general direction of Damon. "But you're my doc now. So, what do you say?"

"Five days. You're still very—"

"No fucking way am I staying five days. I have things to do. You just rethink that right now."

Dr. Waite looked ready to pop something. Humor suited him, she thought, and wanted to make him laugh more. But she in was no mood to appreciate his sparkling eyes and twitching lips.

"Ten days then. If you continue along those lines, Miss Julie, I can double it until you die of old age. Damon's deal works with me. Would you like to argue with me some more, Julie? I'm sure I could get you completely healthy in say...about three months."

Julie looked at Damon, who was coughing behind his hand. He either had a horrific cold or he too was laughing at her. Julie decided that payback was going to be a real bitch for these two.

"Fine. But if Nurse Becky Bitch steps one foot in this room, I'm not going to be responsible for what happens to her."

"Five days and I'll make sure she stays away. And before you open that pretty mouth, remember that it goes to twenty if you do."

Julie decided that Dr. Waite was going to pay dearly for this. But she wisely kept her mouth shut.

~*CHAPTER THREE*~

Cain stopped by to see his mother the next morning. She was awake and being rude to one of the nurses. Cain neatly slipped in and took the meds from the nurse, who looked ready to cry, and told her that he would take care of it.

"That's her job, you know? Stupid girl should just learn to take a little constructive criticism and learn from it. Not have doctors do her job for her."

Cain handed his mother her pills and wondered about the carton of milk and Danish sitting on her tray. "Whose is this?" He pushed the tray away when she went to reach for it.

"It's mine. Your father brought it to me...hey! That's mine. Damn it, Cain, I was going to eat that."

Cain deposited the Danish in the trash and dumped the milk in the sink before throwing the cup away too. His temper was simmering when he walked back to her bed. "You had surgery yesterday morning. You are on a clear liquid diet and you have him bring you Danish. Un-fucking-believable! If this is how you plan to act while I'm helping you, then you may as well go back to California now. I won't put up with this shit."

"You always did hate your dad. He wasn't all that bad, Cain. He tried to go straight and the system kept at him until he just snapped. I would think, as his only son, you'd have more compassion for him. He is your dad, you know."

Cain had heard this all before. From the time he was old enough to know better until he was able to get away, his mother had been defending Roscoe Waite.

"Yes, Mother. It was always everyone else's fault but his. I'm sure prison wasn't his fault either. That man he killed by driving up onto the sidewalk—I suppose that wasn't his fault either?" Cain bit the inside of his cheek before he said anything else. He waited until after she was taken to physical therapy before he left to see his patient. This room was in direct contrast to the one he'd just left.

Where his mother's room was filled with light and a television blaring, Julie's room was dark and quiet. Guinevere Waite's room was filled with flowers and even a basket of fruit that she would never eat. Julie's was bare. Cain thought that Julie's was more welcoming—well, except for the girl, of course. He smiled.

Julie was sitting in a chair when he walked in and she was crying. The nurse making up her bed was talking to Julie, though Cain thought "talking" was a very subjective term for what she was doing.

"...take a bath because you stink. I think I've smelled dirty diapers with a sweeter odor than you have. And how you keep the lice out of your hair is—"

"That's quite enough," Cain thundered. He didn't have to look at the name tag to know this was the dreaded Becky. "You ever treat my patients like I just heard again and I'll have you fired so fast your head will spin. And why is Julie in a chair? I gave specific orders for her to be on bed rest for the next two days."

When Becky Noose didn't answer, Cain turned to Julie. She was pale and he could see the pain etched on her face.

"She said she wasn't touching my skanky ass no matter what some old fart told her to do. She also –"

"Shut up, you stupid bitch before I—"

"Before you what? Don't move from that spot." Cain stepped into the hall and stopped the first nurse he saw. "Could you find Damon Grant for me and tell him I need him stat? Also, your charge nurse, please. Tell them both to meet me in this room."

With a hurried, "yes, sir," she was off. Cain stepped back into the room just as Nurse Becky was drawing back to hit Julie. But before Cain could intercede on Julie's behalf, Becky was on the floor and Julie was standing over her.

"Take that, you fucking bitch." She staggered a little then said, "fuck," and was falling to the floor.

Damon stepped into the room in time to see Cain rolling Julie off Becky. Cain glared at him when the older man laughed.

"She actually tried to hit her. This Becky person tried to hit my patient! I want this girl fired today, Damon. She was going to hit a patient after she'd made her sit in a chair to make her bed."

Cain picked up Julie and waited for Damon to finish the bed before laying her into it. Blood, fresh and dark, spread across her gown. While Cain took the padding off the wound, Damon stepped back to the nurse on the floor.

Julie came around while Cain was trying to stop the bleeding. "I thought you sent her in to punish me. I couldn't...I couldn't figure out what I'd done to you. Why you hate me so much," Julie whispered to him.

Cain looked at her and was moved again by her tears. "I don't hate you. I'm sorry she hurt you, Julie. I promise she won't again."

"Yes, she will. Everyone does it. I'm used to it by now. Everyone begins to hate me after a while."

Before he could respond, she closed her eyes and slipped into unconsciousness. Calling Damon over, they worked to get her bleeding stopped. Neither man spoke as they worked, not even when the charge nurse, Molly Shield, walked up and started to help. It took them twenty minutes to put the stitches back in and another fifteen to get her cleaned up again. It looked like Julie would be staying the ten days after all.

Cain was seething with anger. While he paced outside Molly's office waiting for his turn to speak, Damon sat calmly in the chair. Cain had never run across anything like this in his entire career.

"Cait, my sister-in-law, is on her way in. As Chief of Surgery, I'm pressing criminal charges against Rebecca Noose. Cait will need to take your statement too," Damon said as he leaned back in the plastic chair.

"All right. What do you suppose is going on in there? You think Noose will talk her way out of this?" Cain hoped the hell not.

"No. Molly's good at her job. It was only a matter of time before Nurse Noose got in over her head. I'm just glad that it was Julie that she messed with and not someone who couldn't defend against her."

Cain didn't want to point out that Julie shouldn't have been able to defend herself either. But he did understand what Damon had meant. Cain still couldn't believe that Julie had punched that nurse like that. He chuckled.

"I'd hate to mess with Julie when she is at full strength. I'm betting she'd hold her own against anyone. Including me." Cain sat next to his mentor and friend. "Julie thought I had sent Noose in to punish her. She thought that I hated her." He wanted to go back to Julie's room and make sure she was all right. He wondered at that then decided it was because she was his first patient since moving here from Maine. When the door opened and Molly motioned for them to enter, both men stood.

The office was plush. There were four chairs in front of the desk. Becky Noose sat in one, Damon in one over with a space between, and Cain next to him on the end. Molly's phone rang before they could begin.

"I'm sorry, I have to take this," she told them as she picked up the receiver.

The wall behind the desk was covered in photos. Most of them were of people, lots of kids. But there were a few landscapes, vacation pictures he was sure. Two of them he was sure were of Martha's Vineyard. The wall to the left was covered in ceiling to floor book shelves. There were more pictures here, but mostly there were books. The wall to their right was also shelves, but these held treasures. Cain knew they were treasures because of the way they'd been displayed. He also knew that Molly had a story about each item there and she would know the dates and the people involved with each one.

"That was Human Resources. They will need to sit in on the rest of this. I hope Julie will be all right, Dr. Waite," Molly said as she hung up.

Cain nodded. To be honest, he wasn't sure if he would be able to stop at "yes, she will." The girl beside them looked positively happy about this whole thing.

The door opened a few minutes later. The man who walked in had a file in one hand and a cup of coffee in the other. Cain didn't think this was going to go well. Damon, when Cain looked at him, looked...well, bored. Before anything could be said, Cait Grant walked in.

"This is a closed meeting. You'll have to wait in the—"

"I asked Captain Grant here. She is going to take Julie's statement after she takes Doctors Waite's and Grant's." Molly reached into her drawer and pulled out a plastic bag with a specimen cup inside. "Becky, you'll need to take a drug test. It's just a formality."

"Drug test? For what, may I ask? This is just a case of a misunderstanding. It's my understanding that the woman

Becky...err Nurse Noose supposedly hit is nothing more than a homeless person."

Before Cain could stand up and punch Mr. HR in the nose, Damon put his hand on Cain's arm to stop him. He bristled. If this was the way this hospital worked, he wasn't so sure he wanted to work here.

"Becky, take the test or Captain Grant will take you to the emergency room to draw blood. When there are damages done to the hospital property, a blood or urine test needs to be performed." Cain wasn't sure, but he thought Molly was enjoying this.

"What damages? I hadn't touched her yet and she punched me before I could. There weren't no damages. What?" Becky snarled at HR representative Donald Chesterfield when he reached for her arm.

Cain laughed. He couldn't help it. Not only had Noose admitted to hurting Julie, but in front of witnesses too. And Mr. Chesterfield seemed to of known all about it.

"Becky, either take the drug test or I have no recourse but to terminate you pending a full investigation," Molly said. This time, Cain was sure Molly was enjoying it. The humor in her voice was very evident. When she shook the plastic bag, Cain started to laugh again.

When Noose leaped at Molly, Damon was knocked into Cain. He tried to steady himself, but with the combined weight of Chesterfield and Damon, Cain couldn't move. But Cait Grant had no such trouble.

Before the men were completely untangled, Cait was reading the nurse her rights and cuffing her. Molly was just putting her desk to rights when Chesterfield stood up to leave. That's when Damon stood as well.

"Donald Chesterfield, it is with great pleasure that I terminate you. I have it on good authority that you have been falsifying company records for over a year where Miss

Noose is concerned. Then there is the added charge of theft with intent to distribute."

"No. No, you can't fire me. I'm needed. I have to...who told you? Whoever it is lied. I demand to know who said anything." Cain looked at the man in amazement as spittle ran down his chin.

"I did," Molly said as she sat back down. "I told Damon three weeks ago that I caught you having sex with Becky in one of the rooms. Did you forget the cameras, Donald? Shame on you! And with a patient right in the next bed. Anyway, after that, we had you under surveillance the entire time you were here."

Two armed police walked in as Molly was finished speaking. Donald, AKA Mr. HR, sobbed all the way out the door. Cain sat in stunned silence.

"Well, that was fun. And a lot more eventful than I thought it would be. Thanks, Molly. Coming, Cain?"

Cain looked at Damon as he smiled at Cain. "You planned this? Both of you, you planned this whole thing?"

"Sort of. Not with Julie, but with the drug test. Today just happened to be the way we got to do it. We've been waiting for Noose to take her rage out on someone else before we could act. She's been too clever for us to actually catch her up until now."

Cain looked at Damon. "Please tell me that you didn't send Noose into Julie's room to make this happen?"

Damon looked back at him in shock. "Never! I know you would never ask that if you weren't so stressed. Your mother, is she all right?"

Cain looked at Molly. She would probably find out sooner or later anyway. "My father is here. He's been visiting her. He actually brought her a Danish and milk this morning."

Damon looked at Molly. "Cain's mother is on the surgical floor. His...father was just released from prison. He isn't a very nice person."

Cain thought that was a gross understatement.

~CHAPTER FOUR~

Julie woke to a strange room. It was very nice and filled with flowers. Moving very slowly, she rolled to her back and saw that not only were there flowers and a huge basket of fruit, there was a woman curled up in a chair. She was sleeping in the room's recliner. Julie pulled the call button for the nurses' station, but kept an eye on the woman. The noise of the nurse answering woke the woman up.

"Yes, Miss Julie. What may I do for you? Actually, a nurse will be in shortly."

"But I..." Julie was about to pull the cord again when the woman spoke. She was pretty and wearing very nice clothes.

"They'll be working very hard to make sure you're happy and satisfied. I'm here to make sure of that. I'm Ronnie Grant, by the way."

"Where am I and how the hell do I get out of here?" Julie never panicked. But she was somewhere she couldn't control with people she didn't know.

"Cain said to tell you he'll be in to see you soon. It's all right, Julie. Everything is going to be fine." The voice seemed to be coming from a long tunnel.

Julie's air felt cut off. She couldn't seem to breathe and her heart felt ready to explode. The room seemed ready to close in on her and she tried to draw a deep breath to scream.

Suddenly, someone grabbed her chin and jerked her face around.

"Look at me. Damn it, Julie, look at me. Breathe. In and out. That's it, in and out." Cain, Dr. Waite, was yelling at her. Again.

When she closed her eyes, Julie heard him say something sharp to her. "Stay with me, damn it!"

"You know you have a really shitty bedside manner. Let go of me, you oaf. What the hell am I doing in someone else's room?" When Cain laughed at her, she glared at him. She didn't find any of this the least bit funny. When she looked at the chair, the woman Ronnie was sitting down again. Julie flushed with embarrassment.

"You are in your room. Are you hungry? I still have you on a clear diet, but if you do all right with it, I'll upgrade you to more tomorrow."

When Cain reached out and took her wrist, she tried to pull away, but he was stronger. It was then that she realized he was taking her pulse. She figured it would be back to normal in about a month.

"When can I leave?" Julie asked when he was finished. "I'm not going to be able to afford this room, so whoever authorized this is going to be in big trouble." Julie was already paying the hospital all she could afford each week, but this room was way more than she could manage.

"The room isn't costing you anything, Ms. Julie. That's what I was saying before. I have a form here for you to sign." The papers were suddenly in front of Julie from Ronnie. "This says that you won't sue the hospital for damages and they won't charge you for staying here. Ever. Or I come down on their asses so hard you'd never be hurting for money again."

"I don't need their charity. And I certainly am not hurting for money. Thanks, but no thanks. I'm not buying whatever it is you're selling." Julie looked at Cain, who as still sitting on the bed. "I asked when I could leave. You didn't answer. That's a really bad habit you have, by the way."

When Cain laughed again, she wanted to hit him. She had no idea why he got on her nerves. Before she could tell him anything, Ronnie spoke up. Julie wasn't happy with her apparent humor either.

"This isn't charity, Ms. Julie, I assure you. It's compensation. They don't want you to sue them for the mistreatment you received four days ago. Ms. Noose attacked you and the hospital feels responsible. This is their way of saying they're sorry."

"Look, I just want to—four days ago! I've been here four days? Are you flippin' kidding me? I have to get out of here. Where are my...why are you constantly laughing at me?" She asked Cain. "Do I have a sign on me that you find particularly humorous?" She couldn't seem to make this man understand she was pissed without him laughing all the time. Though she had to admit, he was beautiful when he laughed.

"No, not that I can see. But you are a delight. You will be here another few days at least. When Noose sat you in the—"

"Are you nuts? I need to leave. I have...there are people who depend on me to be there for them." When Ronnie and Cain exchanged looks, Julie knew something had happened. "Tell me. What is it? Something happened and I demand you tell me."

"I'm sorry, Julie, there isn't a nice way to tell you this. Rodney Kincaid passed away several days ago. There wasn't anything you could have done. He was old and he died in his box. The police found him yesterday. Molly came to tell me last evening," Cain told her.

Rodney. Her very good friend Rodney was dead. Julie leaned back against her pillow, tears running unchecked down her cheeks. "He helped me. When I first got...he helped me to become nothing. I never would have made it without him. He was my friend." Julie took a tissue that was thrust at her. "I'd like to be alone now, please."

Julie didn't look to see if they left. She knew when she was alone again. Julie had been on her own for a long time and enjoyed the quiet and the feelings it gave her. She looked at the basket of fruit and thought of her first day of hiding.

"You let anyone know you got yourself a fancy phone and somebody will slit your throat for it. Best if you take it apart and trash them parts around to different dumpsters if you don't want anyone to find you for a time," a voice from a nearby box said.

Smiling, Julie remembered for the first time in years that her name wasn't Julie at all. Her name was Alyssa, Alyssa Marie Howard.

The phone in her hand had rung as she talked to the man who'd just rolled out to look up at her. They were just outside the restaurant her mother, uncle, and brothers were eating at. She'd staggered out the back door through the kitchen. She looked at the caller ID then at the man. She could barely focus on either.

"It's my mom." Julie looked at the ID again. "I can't do it. I won't do what they want. It's sick. Not anymore and not ever again will I answer to them." She broke the phone in half and took out the battery. But before she could do much more than that, she staggered again and fell to the ground. She wasn't sure what happened after that. The man, Rodney he'd told her at one point, took the broken pieces from her and pulled her into his box.

"Come here and sit with me, kid. I'll tell you how to become nothing."

Julie remembered not feeling any fear of the older man. She'd felt safe and secure for the first time in two weeks.

Since her father had died. And now, ten years later, she was alone again.

Julie woke sometime later and realized she wasn't alone in the room. Before she could call out, she smelled the familiar perfume.

"I'm so sorry about Rodney, Molly. He was...he was my best friend. I'm so sorry."

"Thank you. He loved you very much too. He was so much better with you around to care for. Though I'm not sure who cared for whom. I feel like you gave him back to me. I can't thank you enough for that."

Julie nodded. Tears hot and fresh trailed down her cheeks. "Rodney said you were his one true love. He often told me he wished he could have done better by you. I have some of his things. Nothing that he wouldn't want you to have, I assure you. We each...we kept things for each other. Just in case something happened to either of us," Julie told Molly.

Molly got up and walked over to some of the flowers in the window shelf. She was fingering a small flower when she spoke again.

"I know who you are and what you are. He said, Rodney said that someday you'd have to remember that too. He said that you'd be a better woman than the child you were."

Julie felt the room closing in again. If Molly knew, then who else knew? And most importantly, how had Rodney found out?

"What do you want? I assure you, I have no money. Since I left, all I had is long gone." As soon as the words left her mouth, Julie regretted them. Molly turned and looked at her. Julie could see that she had hurt her. "I'm sorry. I shouldn't have...I'm so very sorry."

Molly sat back down and pulled her purse into her lap. She got up and handed an envelope to Julie. She didn't say anything for a few minutes then looked at Julie in the eye. "Rodney wanted you to have that. He brought it to me about a month ago. He asked me not to look at it, but he did give me a file on you. Did he ever tell you what he did before he decided to go into the streets?"

"Yes. He said he was a cop. He told me that he'd killed someone and though it was ruled justified, it wasn't to him. He said it was a small boy. That he'd pulled a gun on Rodney and fired. Rodney returned fire before he saw who it was. He said the little boy was eight."

Molly wiped at her tears. "Yes. He'd be your age about now. Rodney was a good man. He just couldn't forgive himself." She walked to the door, but stopped and turned back to Julie. "The funeral is day after tomorrow. Dr. Waite said you could go, that he would release you by then. It's a graveside, Glenview Cemetery at one o'clock."

The door closed quietly behind her. Julie rolled to her side, buried her face in the pillow, and sobbed for her friend and mentor. Holding the envelope close to her chest, Julie fell into a fitful sleep.

~CHAPTER FIVE~

Cain watched his mother preen. He hadn't ever used that word before, but knew without a doubt that was exactly what she was doing. He'd been in her room for nearly twenty minutes now waiting to take her to her small apartment. He didn't tell her he'd bought Devin and Ronnie's house. He looked at his watch again. Just as he was about to say something to her about his schedule, the door behind him opened.

"Hello, son. How are you? I've been trying to get in touch with you for a month now. You too good to come and see your old man? A man has a right to his family, you know."

Cain looked at the man who was his father and then to his mother, who was smiling at him. His mother hadn't been getting ready to leave, she'd been stalling.

Cain slipped his jacket on. He walked to the door when his father stepped in front of him. Cain had to take a step back.

"Don't touch me," Cain growled between his clenched teeth. "I'm not six anymore and I will fight back. Get the fuck away from me and don't contact me again."

"I paid my debt to society, son. I'm a—"

"Don't call me son. As far as I'm concerned, you're dead to me. Mother, when and if you get smart and he's gone..." Cain pointed to his father. "Give me a call. But not before then."

Cain stood outside his mother's room and leaned against the wall. He couldn't believe she'd done that again. But then, his mother had always been blind by Roscoe Waite. Not even thinking about where he was going, Cain found himself outside of Julie's room. Before he could change is mind, he walked in.

"Julie," he heard Molly say to what appeared to be an empty room. "I doubt anyone is going to care if you smell like a 'shit hole,' whatever that might be. You told me you took a shower. What the problem?"

"I smell like sick people. I did take a shower, though that stupid hose thingy fell on my head twice." Cain didn't say anything when Molly put her fingers to her lips. "Where did you get this dress anyway? It's really...I know it's supposed to be, but it's very girly, isn't it?"

"It's my daughter's. And yes, it's supposed to be girly. Are you about done in there? We need to get going."

The funeral. Cain had forgotten it was today. He'd signed Julie's release papers last night thinking he'd be too busy with his mother today to get her out on time. Now he found himself suddenly free to go. When the door opened from the bathroom, he wasn't sure who was more shocked, Julie at finding him there, or him. Christ! She was a beautiful woman.

"You're lovely," was all he could say. When she turned to look behind her, Cain was suddenly standing in front of her. He brushed her hair from her damp cheek.

"It's the dress," she explained huskily. "Molly lent it to me. I'm going to Rodney's funeral. I can still go, can't I?"

Cain ran his finger down her cheek to her jaw. She was so soft. He watched as her blue eyes darkened and fluttered close. Lifting her chin slightly, Cain leaned down and brushed his mouth over hers. Gently. When she didn't stop him, he slid his hand to the back of her head and brought her to him, her mouth lush and wet, just inches away. Molly clearing her through startled him. He took a step back, but he didn't let her go. He found that he couldn't and didn't want to examine that too closely.

"I'm so sorry, Cain...Dr. Waite, but we're running behind as it is. Dr. Waite...if you'd like to go, I have plenty of room. I'm not sure who all will be there, but—"

"No! I mean no, he can't go, and he has things he has to do...no way. I'm free after this and I don't...you need to let go of me. Please."

Cain looked at the woman in his arms, well, not quite in his arms, but she was close. Julie really was very beautiful. He wanted to kiss her.

Dark hair, damp from her recent shower, was loose and about to her shoulders. He'd never seen it down, but he could see the curl just waiting to take over her face and head. Her eyes, a blue that defied description, were dark as the deep ocean with hints of purple and gold in them. Right now they were sparkling with her embarrassment. Her lush mouth had him thinking of dark nights with silky sheets crumpled on the floor and moans, deep and sensual. Before when he'd seen her, Julie was dressed in baggy, torn clothes that were clean but ill fitting. Now in a black dress that hugged her body, he could see that her breasts were large and full, her waist tiny. So much so that he was sure he could span it with his fingers touching around her. Her long legs were muscled and well-formed. And long, he thought, long enough to wrap around him when he took her hard and fast. Not taking his eyes from Julie, knowing that she could read the lust, the need in his eyes, and wanting her to, he answered Molly. "I would love to go, Molly. And please, call me Cain. If you ladies are ready to go, I'll get the wheelchair."

"For what?" Julie snapped to attention. "If you think I'm riding in one of those suckers, you can just think again. There isn't any way in hell—"

Cain cut Julie off. "Ride or stay. It's entirely up to you. Hospital policy states you leave in one." He grinned at her.

"And I suppose you always follow the rules?" she asked through her clenched teeth.

"When it suits me. Now, it does." Cain had no idea why he was baiting her so much. Julie practically vibrated with anger. When Molly laughed behind him, he smiled more. Cain found himself wondering if Julie would put this much passion into their love-making. And that thought brought him up short. Sex with Julie? Yes, he thought, that was something he'd like to pursue.

The wheelchair ride was made in silence. Cain wasn't sure what was going on in Julie's head, but he was sure it didn't bode well for him. He found he didn't care, was in fact looking forward to bantering with her more. This was as much fun as he'd had as a kid with his sisters, only much more enjoyable.

Cain made a mental note to himself that he needed to warn his sisters that their father was back in town. He also needed to let them know that their mother was aiding and abetting him in his schemes to see them. All five of his sisters had suffered at their parents' stupidity, but not anymore. Not while he could care for them, they wouldn't.

When they pulled up in front of the cemetery, there were about seventy cars already there. And there were several cruisers lined up along the side of the road close to the grave where people were milling about. Molly looked as confused as both Julie and he were. It wasn't until Cait Grant came toward them that things started to fall into place.

"Rodney was one of ours," Cait said when asked about the people there. "He may have been out of touch for a while, but we never leave a cop on his own at a time like this. I understood him to be a great man. And I'm very sorry for your loss."

"Yes. Yes, he was. He just...he had a lot of his own demons that got the better of him. He just couldn't seem to...he had a hard time forgetting." Molly wiped at the tears on her cheeks. "Thank you for this, Captain Grant."

"It was our pleasure. And please, call me Cait. Captain Grant sounds like I should be old and carrying a large cane. If you will all come this way."

The graveside funeral was with full police honor. The twenty-one gun salute made Julie jump with each firing of the rifles, but Cain folded her into his body and held her. The flag was presented to Molly, who was openly crying as she accepted it. Cain, too, was moved by the ceremony.

Cain drove Molly's car to her house. Cait had also arranged for food and beer to be taken to the house so that people could meet there and talk about their friend. The beer, Cain had been told, was for the cops, old and new, to drink to one of their fallen comrades.

Cain kept an eye on Julie for most of the afternoon. She was starting to fade just after the toast. When she disappeared, he went to find her and found Molly instead.

"She went to lie down in my son's old room. My granddaughter Shannon is in there with her. She's a nurse. Julie will be fine, Cain. You worry too much. How much trouble can she get in as hurt as she is?"

Cain didn't bother answering the last part. Plenty, he was sure. "I should get her. I don't know where she's going from here, do you? And the things at the hospital, what happens to those?" Cain needed to talk to Julie, he realized. She couldn't go back on the streets. Not now.

"Julie had me take the fruit to the VA hospital along with the flowers. I gave her back her clothes yesterday, cleaned and pressed. Was there anything else that you were wondering about? I mean, I didn't see any meds for her or prescriptions now that I think about it." He had given her two, one for pain and the other vitamins. "And as for where she's staying...I'm sorry, I just assumed after seeing the two of you together that she...that the two of you, well, I thought you two were seeing each other."

"No, we...we hadn't gotten that far. I mean she's...shit! She drives me nuts, but I still find myself wanting to be with her. I even find myself aggravating her just to see her temper flare. How stupid is that?"

Molly laughed. "Well, you do flare her up. And of course you want to be with her." She patted his cheek. "Oh look, there's Shannon now. Perhaps she can tell you how Julie is doing."

Cain didn't think so. He could tell by the look on the girl's face that something had happened. Somehow, he knew that Julie was no longer in the house.

"Is Julie out here? I just stepped out to go to the bathroom and Dan's window was opened and she wasn't in there anymore."

Cain wanted to howl out his frustrations. But first, he had a woman to hunt down, and heaven help her when he found her. He was going to lay down some rules as soon as he did. If he found her.

~CHAPTER SIX~

Julie moved along the "homes" of her buddies. They weren't friends, not really. They'd as soon stick a knife in someone's back as to look at them. Some were all right, though. Moon and Toby were two of those she trusted to an extent.

"Miss Rocky, you shouldn't be wandering around this late. Get yourself a corner and stay there," Moon whispered harshly at her. She hadn't even seen him inside of his shelter.

Julie was relieved. After Rodney, she didn't want to lose anyone else. "I got you something. But you have to promise me you won't share or let anyone else know you have it." She handed him a shiny apple from the fruit basket she'd gotten.

"Oh Miss Rocky! This is a treat. Yes, it is. An apple, a whole apple. I gotta share with my man Toby. He likes them too, he does."

Julie pulled out a second one and handed it to Moon. "I got one for him too. Plus, an orange each. Don't go telling anyone. You know what will happen if you do. I don't want anything happening to you."

"Yes, ma'am, they'll steal it. Right outta my hand, they will." He smelled the fruit as though it was manna to him, then looked up at her. "You didn't steal this from someone, did you? They won't be coming after old Moon for it back, will they?"

"No, Moon. It's yours fair and square." She watched as he sniffed it again. "Moon, do you think I could bed down close to here tonight? My place is gone."

Julie stayed with Rodney most nights. They hadn't slept together, but they had protected each other. She wasn't even sure she could go back to their place now. Not yet anyway.

"Yeah. Heard about old Rodney. Police had us all moved around that day. That butthole Sherman had me so mad that Toby had to hold me back some. Wouldn't let us pay our respects or nothing. Shame, that. He was a good man, that Rodney. You stay here with me and Toby. We got us a new house just last week."

Julie looked at his new "home." Someone nearby must have gotten themselves a new freezer and Toby and Moon ended up with a new house out of the deal. She was just getting settled when Toby showed up. He'd gone on for twenty minutes about the apple and orange. When they offered her the whole house in exchange for the fruit, she'd told them it was a gift and not a trade, but thanked them anyway. At sometime well after midnight, they settled down to sleep.

Julie thought about leaving Molly's home. She'd felt bad that she hadn't thanked her. She decided to go by the hospital next week and tell her so. Julie was sure that had she stayed, Dr. Waite would have found a way to keep her from where she needed to be. She couldn't do that, not now, not ever.

The envelope that Rodney had given Molly was a surprise. Not only had Rodney found out who she was, but had also kept tabs on Julie's family. They were still searching for her. Even after all this time.

Alyssa Howard was an heiress. Not just an heiress, but one with a brain. That was what the papers had called her when she'd graduated from Yale at fifteen with a business degree. She'd gone on to Brown University as well. She now had three degrees under her real name and had planned to use them running her daddy's company for him.

Alyssa's father had been grooming her to run the company's holdings when he retired. Howard Incorporated bought companies and buildings, revamped them, then sold them for a profit. They also had several hotels all over the world that catered to the rich, famous, and the small families. When Nathan Howard died suddenly when Alyssa was seventeen, he'd left her everything—over eleven billion dollars in company assets alone. Personal accounts and monies added another five billion, making Alyssa the youngest billionaire in the world.

Alyssa's brothers, Nathan the forth and Robert, both older than her, and their mother, had gotten an allowance. And Shannon and her sons were not happy about it. They were to get just over four hundred thousand a year that they would divide between them. And Alyssa held the purse strings. Samuel, her father's brother, too, was on an allowance, but his had stipulations. Stipulations that he wasn't happy about either.

So when they approached her with their "plan," Alyssa ran. The plan was sick and perverted. Their plan made Alyssa Howard become a nothing.

The clippings that Rodney had saved for her said that there was a reward for anyone knowing about her, living or dead. She didn't have to wonder why Rodney hadn't turned her in for the money. Two million dollars would have gone a long way to comfort most people. But Rodney had been her friend, almost like her father had been to her. Julie wondered what her family would think if they knew their missing daughter slept most nights under their noses.

Looking across the parking lot from where she slept most nights Julie watched the guard walk the perimeter of the Howard Building, not knowing that less than fifty yards away, their boss slept. Julie snuggled down on the cardboard sheet that Toby had found for her and pulled her coat tighter around her. That's when she thought of Dr. Cain Waite.

Cain had kissed her. She'd been kissed before, she'd even had sex a couple of times when in a night of loneliness and stupidity, she'd had a classmate "do her." Julie doubted that Cain would "do her" in quite the same way, neither would it be as clumsy and unsatisfying.

Cain was gorgeous, sweet, and polite. Well, not to her really, but she had seen him around others and knew that he could be. To her, he was bossy, rude, and...well, really bossy. But he had also called her lovely. No one had called her that since her father.

Julie rolled to her back, wincing at the pain. Cain was going to be so pissed when he figured out she had left. Even more so when he figured out where she'd gone. Smiling, she kind of wished she could see the look on his face when he did. Well, she thought, he'd forget about her soon enough. She was where she wanted to be, where she needed to be.

~~~

Cain wasn't mad at Julie, he was furious. The little twit was gone. And not only was she gone, but she was hurt too. When he found her, and he had no doubt that he would, he decided that he was going to paddle her backside but good, then he was going to make love to her until she was too sated, too relaxed to leave him again.

"You know that if she doesn't want to be found, you won't find her, don't you? She has more aliases than I have ever heard. Half the people we talk to won't answer us; the other half have no clue who she is," the cop, Neil James, mused. Cait had assigned him to help Cain look for Julie and he was, frankly, driving Cain nuts.

"I'm going to find her," Cain growled for the third time in the last twenty minutes. "Have you asked those people over there? I'm going to ask them; you go over there and ask."

"Who should I tell 'em we're looking for? I got no idea what to call the stupid girl. Why she'd be out in this sort of weather is beyond me. I'd want to be in my…"

Cain tuned him out. If he didn't, he might choke the life out of the cop. How a person got through life as negative as Neil was beyond Cain. He walked up to the next "house" and knocked on the top.

Cain looked around the area. There were perhaps twenty men and women staying in this area of Columbus. Their homes varied as much as the people living here. Boxes from large appliances, sheets pulled over strings. Two people he'd seen so far were living in a car, the front wheels gone and the back ones flat. Most of the people were dirty and had smelled so bad that Cain was thankful they were out of doors. But others were clean, if not a little worn down.

Cait had told him not to wear nice clothes when coming down here. He'd already figured that out, but he was sure her reasons were vastly different than his had been. He needed to blend in and his suit pants wouldn't have done that. She'd also told him not to take out his cell phone or his wallet, and under no circumstances was he to give anyone money. He'd be killed in a quick breath of air if he did.

Cain could smell the man before he poked his head out of his box. He leaned down to speak to him when he looked as if he wasn't going to come out. That's when he saw the two oranges and the apple. The fruit basket.

Cain wasn't sure how he knew Julie had given this man the fruit, but he did. When the man noticed that Cain was looking at them, he covered the fresh fruit with his blanket and glared up at Cain.

"I don't need no preaching. I get enough of that on Wednesday when I get my free meal at the shelter on

Tuesday. It's Friday now, and I want you to peddle your wares somewhere else."

Cain was slightly confused about the timeline, but hurried on before the man went back into his shelter. "I'll give you two more oranges and a pear if you tell me who gave you those oranges."

The man eyed Cain for what seemed an eternity and just when Cain was about to double the offer, the man spoke. He had a great deal of suspicion in his voice, but he did answer. "Pears are mighty expensive, boy. You must want her real bad. I think maybe you'd go for...three pears and four oranges. I think that's worth some information, don't you?" He smiled up at Cain.

Cain would have bought him a crate of whatever he wanted if he led him to Julie. But now it was a matter of pride and bargaining. He knew the man wouldn't just take the fruit. He'd seen what thinking someone was trying to give charity had made Julie feel.

"All right, but two pears. As you said, they are expensive. And if this is the girl I'm looking for, I'll give you some bananas too," Cain said after careful consideration.

The man looked at his stash then back at Cain. "She in trouble? I like Miss Rocky. She ain't done nothing but be a good girl to me and my Toby. But a man has to eat."

Cain's disappointment was profound. Miss Rocky wasn't who he was looking for. He'd pay the man anyway—a deal was a deal, but he was disappointed all the same.

"No, she's not in trouble. Just...I'm sure Miss Rocky isn't who I was looking for anyway. If you'll wait here, I'll go and get you your payment. You did keep your end of the bargain."

Cain stood. He was tired and thinking maybe Neil was correct. Julie didn't want to be found. He'd been looking for two days now and still nothing. He was about to turn away when the man spoke again.

"Miss Rocky is a good girl, you know. She didn't get mad at me when I cut her up the other week. Scared, I was, having myself a bad dream and all. All she'd been doing was telling me to get my fool self out of the rain. I sliced her belly right open, I did. I quit sleeping with the knife in my hand now. Too dangerous for an old fool like me to do that."

Cain looked around. It was her and he knew it. "Do you know where she is? That's the girl I'm looking for."

"She'll be back directly. Miss Sally, she got herself a nasty cut the other day and Miss Rocky went to take her to the clinic. They'll get nasty with us when we go. Miss Rocky, she gives it right back to them. Funny thing to watch her get all up in their faces like she does." The old man laughed. "Spouting off them rules like she done wrote them."

Cain just bet she did. He nearly smiled, then the anger surged forward. Damned girl. He was going to string her up when he found her. Then he wasn't sure what he was going to do. But she was certainly not going to live here anymore. Cain was about to thank the man when he saw the bane of his misery coming toward him. He was glad that he'd seen her first or she might have run. But he was nearly to her when she looked up. The older woman she was helping was still walking and talking even though Julie had stopped.

"Hello. Are you my Carl?" Cain looked at the older woman again, Sally, the man had called her. "No. No, not my Carl. He wasn't as pretty as you are."

When Julie took a step back, Cain grabbed her arm. "I don't think so, Miss Rocky. You're coming with me. Now."

"I don't want to. I like it here. How did you find me anyway?" Julie asked as she struggled against his grip.

"Oranges. If you try to run, so help me I will chase you down and beat that beautiful ass of yours. I'm in a foul mood and—"

"Well there's a shocker! Cain Waite in a foul mood. You've been in one since I've known you."

He felt his lips twitch. Damned girl. Cain pulled her tight to his body. "Do you think there's a correlation there? You've tested my temper since I've met you."

"See here. You let Miss Rocky go. I don't care how many oranges and pears you bring me. You let her go right now, boy. I will hurt you."

Cain looked at the man coming toward him. His gait was slow but sure and Cain did not want to hurt him. He didn't want to hurt anyone, especially a man protecting the same person he was. But the older man was sporting a bat.

"Julie," Cain growled low. "Tell him to stop. Tell him I'm not hurting you. I don't want to cause any trouble. I just want to take you home with me."

Cain waited and so did the man. Cain never took his eyes off of Julie's face. He was sure of one thing, there was going to be a fight, but he would lay odds it wasn't going to be with the man behind him. She looked ready to do battle and he was sure she would take skin and blood when she was finished.

"It's okay, Moon. I know him. I don't like him or care for him overly much right now, but I know him. I have to go with him for a minute, then I—"

"Moon? You know her, right? I'm trying to get her off the streets. You know this isn't the kind of life for a pretty young woman. You tell her that she needs to come with me, please," Cain said to Moon.

Sally stepped forward. "Oh, dearie, if he wants you to get off the streets, then you should listen to him. He's right. This ain't no life for the likes of you. You'll be worn down in no time and you know that Rodney would want you to. So long as he ain't expecting you to turn tricks...you ain't, are you, young man?"

"No, ma'am, I'm not. I just want her to get off the streets and safe. Just like you do," Cain answered. He suddenly had a thought. He wondered if that was how she had survived all these years. Cain hoped if it had been her way of life, that she had been safe.

"I really, really hate you right now," Julie said as she jerked away from him.

Cain watched as she went back toward Moon's house. He followed her. There was no way he was letting her out of his sight again. Not now that he'd found her.

Cain watched as she gathered up her few things and stuffed them into a plastic grocery bag. She had another pair of pants and a few books. Then she kissed Moon and told him to tell Toby that she'd see them both around. He reached to help her by taking the bag to carry for her. He stepped back when she growled at him. No one had ever growled at him before and it startled him somewhat. Not even that stupid dog they'd had as kids. But he was sure, in that second, he'd never been so afraid. Not that she'd kill him, but he was pretty sure she would hurt a couple of his more...private parts if he tried to reach for it again. He simply pointed the way to his car parked down the street.

Julie didn't say another word to him. Not all the way across the lot of the Howard Building's parking lot nor when he'd opened the car door for her. He did nearly lose his fingers when she jerked her door from him and shut it before he had time to move fast enough. By the time they got to his house, he was pretty angry himself.

~CHAPTER SEVEN~

Julie didn't even wait for Cain to come around and open her car door. But jumped out as if the thing was on fire and she was going to save herself. She had a good mind to set it on fire anyway, damned man. She stomped up the front steps to his house and waited for him, daring him to say a single word to her. Once the door was open, she stalked inside and sat on the floor. She was off the streets, there wasn't any way she was moving in with the idiot.

"Are you planning to be this childish the whole time you live here? If so, this could get really tedious. Come up the stairs so that I can show you your room while you're here."

"No." Julie laid her small collection of books next to her on the floor and then folded her pants on the other side of her. She left her toothbrush and other toiletries inside to use as a carryall.

"Julie, I'm doing this for your own good. You could—"

"Fuck you." Her temper was near meltdown. She had never been so furious in her life. If he thought to make her stay, he was in for a big surprise.

"You aren't making me the bad guy in all of this. You can't expect me to just let you live on the streets like an animal."

That's it! He'd pushed her over the edge just that quickly. She leapt up off the floor as she rushed toward him. "Animal! Animal? Why you arrogant, misguided, overbearing asshole. What give you the right to judge me? Where do you get off thinking you have any say in what I do?" She poked him in the chest. "Where I live?" Another poke. "And how I chose to live?" She poked him again.

When he only stared at her, looking down his nose, she turned away. Furious tears streamed down her cheeks as she gathered up her things. She was leaving and he'd better not even think about trying to stop her.

~~~

Cain seemed to wake up when Julie opened the front door to leave. He only meant to stop her, just to pull her back from the door when she jerked away from him. Their feet got tangled up and they started to fall. Cain moved to shelter her from his weight falling on her and she landed over him as his back hit the floor. The breath whooshed out of his lungs.

They lay there, both breathing hard for several seconds. When Julie sat up, her legs wide over his hips, Cain held her there by grabbing her thighs. When she stilled, he sat up, Julie still in his lap.

Cain watched her eyes as he brought his hands around her to her ass and cupped her, bringing her to his body. When she grabbed onto his shoulders and pressed tighter, Cain raised his hands to her breasts, lifting them, nuzzling the heavy, cloth-covered weight in his hands with his mouth. Biting and nipping through her shirt, he could feel her hardened nipple as it peaked inside of his mouth, and he wanted more. While still feasting, he reached down between them and pulled her shirt up, only moving his mouth away to pull the fabric over her head. Her breasts were bare. And when he pulled her nipple into his mouth, Julie pressed herself tighter to his body.

Julie was riding him now. Her legs wrapped around him after she moved her body up. Cain, never taking his mouth from her nipples, rolled her over and settled himself between her legs, her back on the floor. His cock ached to be released and buried deep inside of her. Shifting slightly, he reached down to the snap and zipper on her jeans and growled when he kept fumbling with them. Sitting up, he nearly ripped them open and moved back to pull them from her legs. Shoes and socks scattered everywhere.

When she lay naked before him, he couldn't move, couldn't breathe. Christ, she was gorgeous. When she sat up, Cain thought for sure she meant to leave him like this, hard and hurting. He was surprised when she grabbed the front of his shirt, ripped it open, took his nipple into her hot mouth, and bit him.

"Christ," he hissed at her. Her growled, "off," and her small hands on his pants snap nearly unmanned him.

Julie had his pants open in no time. Her hot hand wrapping around his cock had him surging against her. Her mouth trailed down his body and nipped at his ribs even as she worked at his pants to get them down.

Need coiled in his belly. Lust so powerful he felt it consume him. Moving forward and over her, she lay back and he slammed into her hard and fast. He shuddered when she arched up under him.

Christ, she was tight. Heat enveloped him, slick and wet. When she wrapped her legs around him and rocked up, he felt his climax roar up and ready to explode. When Julie gripped his waist, nails dug deep, he rocked again and she screamed out her release. Cain couldn't help it. With her body milking him, pulling him deeper into her, he threw back his head and pounded into her through the most powerful orgasm he'd ever had.

Dropping onto her as he rolled them over onto his back, he spread her over him. Cain closed his eyes while waiting for his heart to beat at a normal pace again. When he had more control of his own body, he lifted his head slightly and looked at the woman lying limp over his body. Lifting her chin gently, he heard her soft snore and he smiled.

Maybe, he thought, this was the perfect way to win an argument with her. Fuck her into submission. While he lay there basking in sated glow, he looked where they were.

The front entrance hall to his new home and they'd gotten no further. Even the front door from where she'd tried to leave him was standing open slightly. He was very glad that the house sat on twenty acres. No telling who might have heard them had they been in a town setting, or worse yet, his apartment in Maine. Rolling to his side, laying Julie onto the floor and to her back, he looked down at her.

Her face, relaxed now in sleep, was soft. She spent all her time out of doors and rather than make her look worn, she had a healthy glow about her and rosy cheeks. Her hair he could see now wasn't just dark. It was black, raven black with hints of brown and gold. He knew that it was a natural color. There wouldn't be any way for her to dye something to such a beautiful color.

Cain looked at her nakedness and realized that he would need to be more careful in the future. Whisker burns reddened her tender skin along her breasts and neck. Julie shifted to him slightly and he realized she was probably chilled. Getting up, Cain pulled his pants on, walked to the door, and closed and locked it. Picking up her clothes, he tossed them over his shoulder and then leaned down and picked her up. With a small moan, her arms wrapped around his shoulders and she snuggled deep into his chest. Cain took her to his bedroom before he laid her back on the hard floor, woke her, and made love to her again.

Cain was glad now that he'd bought the house as-is. He'd gotten a really good deal on it. Devin had told him that the furniture was included in the house price because though there was nothing wrong with it, neither he nor Ronnie wanted to have to deal with getting rid of it. He said that they were too busy to find someone to take it.

Laying Julie on the comforter, Cain went to the other side of the bed and pulled down the blankets and sheets for her. Picking her up again, he put her in the bed and covered her up. She immediately rolled to her side facing the middle of the bed. Grinning, he went back downstairs to set the security alarm and lock up the house. He hadn't realized how late it was. At three-thirty in the morning, Cain got into bed with Julie and pulled her tight against his bare body. He fell asleep faster than he'd had in a very long time.

~*CHAPTER EIGHT*~

Julie woke with the sunlight streaming across her face. That was normal enough when she would forget to close up her little area. What freaked her out was the warm body wrapped around her, tight. Moving carefully, she raised up slightly to look at the man who currently had his arm draped around her.

Curls fell over his face as he lay sleeping. His hair was mussed badly and stuck up everywhere. Cain's face was rough. A growth of day old beard sprouted over his cheeks and chin. Rodney had shaved everyday with a straight razor and a bar of soap at the corner gas station. Julie wondered if Cain had had to shave more than once a day.

Looking down at his chest, she realized that she'd been correct about it. A fine dusting of hair covered his chest and narrowed down his tapered waist to just below his navel. Seeing his cock semi-hard against his thigh had her blush. They'd had sex and she was just now seeing his body. And it occurred to her that it had been unprotected sex at that.

Lifting his arm off her, Julie finally rolled out of his bed. She searched the entire room for her pants, but they were either still downstairs in the hallway or he'd thrown them out. She opted for the hallway as his clothes were on the chair by the bed.

Pissed, Julie went to the big closet and pulled one of his dress shirts off the hanger. Grabbing her bag up, Julie left the bedroom quietly.

She wanted a shower in the worst way. Going to the bedroom as far from him as she could, she stepped inside and searched for a bathroom. Opening the door was like stepping into her past life. The room was huge and elegant and looked like hers from when she'd been a teenager trying to fit in with the other girls her age.

The bed, a king-sized with a canopy, was covered in white eyelet lace. There was more of it on the bed and surrounding it. The bed was covered in pillows of all sizes from about four inches square to the three that looked to be as much as a yard square. The four posts at the corner of the bed were also white, as was the rest of the furniture. Bright pink and blue scatter rugs were everywhere over the hardwood floor. A window seat, the curtains open to the morning sun, also had an abundance of throw pillows in the same varying sizes. Bookshelves lined one wall. Empty now, they would have been filled with school girl treasures and photos. The desk, also empty of anything of the girl who had once lived here, was also big and open, perfect for chatting online with friends or doing homework. Walking across the large room, Julie tried to shut out the feelings of loneliness and despair.

The bathroom was white too, including the shower curtain and rug on the floor. The only thing left in here that told something of the previous occupant was the shower curtain hooks. Ducks, yellow and bright, danced across the rod and held up the pristine white curtain.

Turning on the water, Julie pulled out her towel she was seldom without and laid it on the rod near the shower. When the water was just about right, grabbing up her shampoo, toothbrush, paste, and washcloth, Julie stepped into the steamy water. The tears fell almost immediately.

For the first time in a very long time, Julie missed her old self. She missed her daddy and his sense of humor. She missed the cigars he'd sneak around to smoke because her mother had hated the smell. On Sunday mornings before the house woke, they would go to the local pancake place and eat stacks and stacks of them with sausage links and orange juice.

The first Sunday after he'd died, Julie went to their old place and sat in their favorite spot, right up at the counter, and ordered a plate for them both. When she'd eaten the very last bite and drank the last of her juice, she paid her bill and never returned. She wondered then if she would ever be able to return there. She knew that right now if she had the money, she'd go again just to have a plate for her daddy. Go on his birthday and have a steak for him as well.

Feeling foolish, Julie finished her shower and stepped out. Drying herself a little too roughly, she noticed the small red places on her skin and once again, thought about how they'd gone at each other last night. She winced at the cut on her belly. It was healing nicely, but was tender yet. She had to go to the clinic soon and get...she thought of the man down the hall, the naked man down the hall in the bed, warm and hard. His body—

Julie pulled on Cain's shirt and refused to think about him again as she pulled on her last pair of clean panties. She was all the way to the door and had just put her hand on the knob when someone knocked, scaring her enough to have her jump back in alarm.

When the person on the other side knocked again, Julie had her wits back enough to know that if that person woke the man upstairs, she was a good as stuck here. Shouting to the person to hang on, Julie looked at the security panel to the right of the door. Smiling, she read Cain's note on how to arm and disarm the locks. Keying in the code, she opened the door and was nearly knocked over by the woman just on the other side.

"Thank God! What the fuck took you so...you're not Cain. Shit! Is this his house or am I lost again? Great!"

"Take a deep breath before you pass out. And I'll have you know, you couldn't have been standing here for more than ten seconds—took so long indeed." Julie looked at the woman and then the two suitcases she had with her. "Moving in, huh? Good, I'm about to leave."

Before Julie could grab her own bag, the woman grabbed her arm. "Are you nuts? He's out there. I tried to lose him, but he's had a lot of practice at hiding in the dark."

Julie watched the woman pace when she had released her arm. Julie wanted to be gone before Cain woke up. Long before he realized she was missing again. Before she could tell the woman she was out of there, someone else knocked on the door.

"What is this, Grand Central Station? Sheesh." Since the code was already turned off, Julie tore the door open, ready to blast the person on the other side.

Another woman, with a single suitcase this time, stood on the stoop. "Oh thank goodness you made it," she said in way of greeting. "I thought for sure he was going to catch me for a second or two." The woman turned toward Julie and smiled. "Hello."

"Hey. Well, since you both seem to know each other then—"

The door flew from her hand and knocked the second woman down. Before Julie could get up, a man grabbed the first woman and slapped her hard across the face. Blood erupted from her nose. Julie jumped up, fighting dizziness, tore the guy away from her and punched him in the nuts. Usually that at least slowed a man down, but this guy simply slapped her.

Julie picked up the first thing she could get her hands on and hit him with an umbrella. All it did was knocked him down and away from the woman he'd managed to hit a second time. Julie had just enough time to jump on his back, grab a hand full of his hair, and yank him back again, tossing him to the floor, her astride his back.

Julie took a deep breath, her body aching and sore. She looked at the woman, her lip bloodied and her eye swollen, but she seemed fine. Julie hadn't realized that the second woman had been hurt when the door had slammed against her head, creasing her forehead.

"Are you all right?" Julie asked the first woman. At her nod, Julie looked at the second woman again. "Can you check on that other one? I think he hit her with the door."

"I did fucking not! A man has a right to see his own kids. You get the—" Julie slammed his head on the tiled floor, hard and quick. "You fucking bitch. You wait until—" This time, his head hit hard enough to knock him out.

"She's breathing well and her pulse is strong. Do you know Cain? And where he is?"

Instead of answering her, Julie got up, but came back down hard. She wasn't just dizzy now, but sick with it. "Can you go scream for him? He's in the bedroom to the left at the end of the hall. I'm just...I'm just going to sit here for a minute then leave you three to sort this out. Well, four of you to sort it out." Julie watched the woman come toward her. If she wanted to finish her off, Julie was pretty sure she'd let her.

"You saved us. The least I can do is help you to a chair. Come on. I'm Jazzie, by the way."

Julie felt the room sway slightly then mercifully settle. The next thing she knew, her head was between her knees and she was looking at the floor.

"Stay that way until I get back with Cain. You move and I'll be really pissed. I mean it."

The woman even sounded like Cain, bossiness and all. At the woman's, "thanks", Julie realized she'd spoke out loud.

"That wasn't supposed to be a compliment," she shouted after her. Julie knew the woman heard her. Her laughter could be heard all the way down the hall.

The woman had to be Cain's wife. No other explanation for it. She glanced over at the woman on the floor. And she had to be her sister. Julie felt dizzy all over her body this time. She'd had unprotected sex with a married man in this very hall not twenty-four hours ago. Grabbing her bag after making sure the man was still out, she walked out the opened door and to the stairs. She didn't get any further than the top step before she had to sit down again. Damn it.

~~~

Cain was sound asleep when a scream rent the air. Jumping out of bed, his first thought was for Julie. And she was gone. When another scream sounded, he threw open the door, fists at the ready.

"Damn it, Cain. She didn't tell me you were naked. But now that I think on it, she didn't have that many clothes...do you think you could put that thing away? It's very early in the morning for that sort of show."

"Jazzie? What the hell? Where's Julie? Damn it, if she's gone again I'm—"

"Cain! Focus! You're buck fucking naked. Sister here! Put something over that thing."

Cain turned and went back into his room. Pulling on his jeans, he nearly tore his dick off when he yanked the zipper up too hard. Picking up his shirt, he went back into the hall.

"You'd better have a good reason for coming here at five in the morning. And where is Julie? You didn't answer me before." Cain kissed his sister's cheek.

"If you mean that pretty woman with the dark hair, she was sitting in the hallway with her head between her knees. I've called the police. This is a really nice house."

Cain had just awakened. He'd not had a shower, brushed his teeth, or had anything to eat so he was reasonably sure he'd missed something. He was halfway down the stairs when he realized that Jazzie had said she'd called the police and by then he could hear the sirens.

Roscoe Waite was just coming around when Cain entered the hall. Quinn was still sitting on the floor, but she said she was all right.

"Where's that fucking girl? She's gonna get sued after I'm finished with her. She had no reason for knocking a man out in his own son's house. Cain, you see to me first. Quinny said she was all right. Look at what she did do me."

Cain ignored his father and looked at Quinn, then at Jazzie. Quinn had a knot on her forehead that would be painful for a while and Jazzie had a busted lip that could use a couple of stitches and her eye was bruised. He was just going to look for Julie when the police knocked on the door frame to his open door.

"Do you know this young woman, Dr. Waite? She claims she was just passing by and sat down to enjoy the view. I think she might be hurt too," the officer said, humor evident in his voice.

"Yes. She belongs to this bedlam. This man—" Cain pointed to his father. "He does not."

Cain picked up a protesting Julie and sat her down on the couch in the living room. Every time she started to rise, he pushed her back down again. Finally, he leaned down to her and whispered in her ear.

"Get up again and I will pull you across my knees and beat your ass. I'm not in the best of humor right now."

"Well neither am I. And you just try it, buster, and I'll tell your wife what we did where she is currently standing."

Cain was too furious with her to explain. His sisters had been hurt, as well as Julie, by his father. It was all he could do not to pound the man into the floor. The only thing going through his head was the amount of witnesses there were in the room.

"Miss Waite, I have a report that says this man here isn't supposed to be within a hundred yards of you. That true?" Officer Tanner, Jake, he'd said, asked Jazzie.

"Yes. One hundred yards or he goes to jail. If this young lady hadn't punched him in his balls, he might have really hurt us all. It happened so fast."

Cain looked at Julie who was trying to pull a pillow over her belly. Dropping to his knees in front of her, Cain fought her, trying to get the pillow from her.

"Do you have to make everything we do a fight? Damn it, Julie, let me see." Cain glared right back at her when he noticed she was glaring.

She hit him with it. "You know, I think I might have mentioned this before about your bedside manner. You might think about taking an anger management course or something." He pinched her thigh to shut her up. "Ouch! You ass, that hurt."

Cain could hear his sisters laughing at him. The sound was so unexpected and long-forgotten that he ignored that they were having fun at his expense. "Jake, would you mind handing me my medical bag from the front closet? Julie has pulled some stitches and I want to make sure they don't need to be put back in."

"I'm not hurt, I was covering myself up, you idiot. Will you please go play in the street and leave me alone?" She pulled the pillow back onto her lap.

As soon as the officer left the room, Cain cupped both hands on Julie's face and kissed her. It was quick and hard, but it left them both slightly breathless. "Julie, this is Quinn and the other one in the chair behind me is Jasmine or

Jazzie. They're my sisters. Well, two of them anyway. The man the police are taking away, that's our father."

Cain didn't look up when he heard her draw a sharp breath, but continued to examine her wound. He hated his father more in that moment than he had all his life. When Julie lifted his chin with her finger, she was smiling.

"I thought they were, well, that one, Jazzie, I thought she was your wife," Julie whispered to him. It was low, but Jazzie could hear.

"Ewww, gross! Seeing him buck naked today was bad enough to scar me for years. Even the thought of...just too gross to think about again."

"You saw him naked? Cool! I saw Gracie naked once. But she was a teenager and a girl. Probably not the same, I think. But Cain? Yeah, ewww written all over that," Quinn said.

Cain turned to glare at his sisters. "She's my twin." He inclined his head toward Quinn. "But I'm older and she should have more respect."

Julie snorted. "Respect is something you earn. You"—she smacked Cain's shoulder—"are a royal pain in the ass. I can see the resemblance now. But I'm assuming she got all the niceness and you got...well, all the sarcasm. And then some."

Both his sisters burst out laughing. "Oh, I like her. Can we keep her?" Jazzie asked.

"No. I have a life of my own. Thanks. And as soon as I can convince this—"

"Your bag, doc. Mr. Waite is on his way downtown. But if he can post bail, he'll be out again in a few hours. You might want to have those gates out front locked up from now on," Jake said.

"Thanks, Jake. It was on my list of things to do today," Cain said, feeling guilty he'd not done it quicker.

"I just need to get everyone's name for the report to file."

Jake looked at Julie first. Cain did as well. She was pale and Cain was sure she was panic-stricken. He had hoped to get her real name and this seemed to be the perfect opportunity. But her face, her expression, said she wasn't giving it up. When she looked at him, Cain knew for a certainty that she was hiding from someone.

"Quinn, take Jake in the kitchen for me, please? I need to have a word with Julie." Cain never took his eyes from hers. "Use this address as your home base and tell Jazzie too."

"Okay. Jake? It's doubtful, but let's see if there's some coffee on. Can you believe it? Cain doesn't drink it. Then there's..." The door closing to the kitchen cut her off.

"Tell me who you are, Julie."

~CHAPTER NINE~

Julie looked at him. She thought she could trust him, but wasn't one hundred percent sure yet. So many people were greedy and she could make someone a very rich person fast if her family found her. She leaned back on the couch and looked around the room.

The room was a beautiful mixture of antiques and modern stuff. The blends of bright colors and dark woods gave the room a very homey, cheerful feel that Julie was certain could be changed easily to formal if need be. She was just thinking about the fireplace when Cain spoke again.

"Julie?"

"I'm not...I won't tell you. Him either. I've worked too hard at becoming who I am. If I have to run again to avoid this, I will."

Cain stood up and walked to the fireplace she had just been admiring. With a flick of a switch, there was a roaring fire warming the chilled room. She could feel the heat and was afraid that it all wasn't coming from the fireplace.

"You don't trust me." It wasn't a question, but she answered anyway.

"I trusted only one person in my life and he's dead. People who I should have been able to trust betrayed me more than I thought would have been possible. You've known me for a very short time and I've no reason to not trust you. Nor do I have any reason to trust you."

Cain didn't say anything for a long while. He just stared into the flames. "Is your real name Julie? Or any of the other four or five names I've heard you called when I was looking for you?" he asked without raising his head.

"No. Julie was a name one of the older ladies called me because she thought I was her daughter."

"Sally," he guessed.

It took her a second or two to remember that he'd seem them together. "Yes. Sally. Miss Rocky is because Moon, the man I gave the fruit to, calls me that because of Rodney. Moon thought Rodney's name was Rocky. I don't believe Moon is right in the head most days. He sometimes has nightmares about his time in the war and I don't think he knows the difference when that happens to him. I got the name Shade because someone thought I was a 'shade short on sense' to be living out there." Julie looked at Cain. "I suppose he was right."

Cain continued to stare at the flames. Then seemingly coming to some decision, he turned and looked at her. Julie waited for his anger.

"We had unprotected sex. There could be a child because of it. Are you...do you...how much sex have you had with strangers? Am I safe?"

Cain wanted to know if she hooked. And for as much as she was hurt by his question, she couldn't really blame him. She could understand his concern even, but it hurt nonetheless. She stood up. "I don't do drugs, not even to smoke pot. I had sex three times if you count us fucking on the floor like the animal you accused me of being. The other two times was when I was sixteen, both with the same boy and both times with a condom." She straightened his shirt over her body. "I'd like my clothes, please. I want to leave here. Now."

Cain looked ready to say something, but he door flew open and there stood an older woman with Jazzie right behind her. Jazzie was crying and the older woman looked furiously at her. Julie went to Jazzie. Cain stopped her.

"We aren't finished here."

Julie turned to look at him. "There was never a 'we,' Doctor Waite. Excuse me," she said as she brushed past the older woman and out the door. She heard Cain ask what the other woman, his mother, wanted before Julie shut the door behind her.

Julie led Jazzie to the kitchen with her arm around her shoulders. She just let the girl cry. Julie needed to get out of here. When they entered the kitchen, Quinn was seated at the table reading a paper. She looked up when she heard them.

"I told you to let me take her in. She'll probably ask Cain for the money for the prick's bail too." Quinn smirked. "Knowing Cain, he won't give it to her either."

Julie filled the pot on the stove with water and turned the burner on. She hadn't had a cup of tea in ages and had no idea why she wanted one now. While the water boiled, she took down three mugs and put them near the stove. Finding some Earl Grey, she put a bag into each cup and set the sugar on the counter. When she finished, she turned, and both women were staring at her.

"What?" she asked embarrassed.

"You're living with Cain? That's so...well, you're so...so, you and Cain, huh?" Quinn asked with a smile.

Julie didn't like the smile, nor did she care for the way they were looking at her. Like they'd just won the lottery and she was the grand prize or something. "No, we had sex. Once. And for some reason, he believes I need for him to boss me around." Julie opened the doors under the sink and looked in the trash.

"Yeah, that's Cain. He's very protective. I guess because he's the oldest. And the only boy. He protected us girls as much as he could while we were growing up." Quinn got up and poured the hot water into the cups when Julie walked away.

Julie opened the cabinets, vaguely noting they were well stocked. "Well, I don't want or need his protection. I do just fine on my own, thanks." She closed the last one as she finished speaking.

"He doesn't listen. He thinks...what the hell are you looking for?"

Julie looked at Quinn when she asked. "In case it has escaped your notice, I'm slightly under dressed here. I know he hid my clothes somewhere just to make sure I wouldn't escape. But if I don't find them soon, I don't give two shits what I don't have on. I'm outta here."

"You want to...okay. I have some clothes you can wear. They aren't much, just some jeans and t-shirts." Quinn picked up her suitcase and began pulling out clothes.

Julie watched her, amazed someone could get that many clothes in one small case. She had more clothes in her case than Julie had owned over the past five years. Her thoughts made her angry. She loved her life now. Then she thought of something.

"What happened to the cop? He seemed hell bent for...you didn't kill him, did you?" Julie was kidding and they all three laughed.

"No. Tempting, but no, I didn't. He asked me out if you can believe it. Here, these should work for you." Quinn handed her an arm load of clothing, most of it in very bright colors. "I told him you were hiding from an ex-husband who had hurt you and he had access to certain files such as police information. I saw them do that on one of those crime shows on television the other night. Wouldn't you know it, it worked!"

Julie took the clothes to the small bathroom just off the kitchen. She held up the shirts one at a time trying to find the one that had the least amount of color in it. Each shirt had so many bright colors and designs that Julie was sure come cockatoo had been the inspiration for them. Pulling one over her head, she immediately tugged it from her body. She wasn't used to things actually fitting her. After pulling on the jeans, also too tight, she continued to tug at the shirt as she returned to the kitchen. Cain and his mother were standing there as well. It wasn't until she heard Jazzie telling how Julie had hit Mr. Waite that she entered the room.

"You hit my husband? Who the hell do you think you are going around beating on poor, helpless men? He's paid his debt to—"

"Mother, shut up. Jul...she's a guest in this house and you'll be nice. This is my mother, Guinevere Waite. This is...this is a friend of mine, ours. She was living on the streets when I found her."

Julie felt the tears begin to burn. She looked at Mrs. Waite and nodded. She didn't trust herself to speak. Instead, she went to the drawer she'd found earlier filled with empty grocery bags. She pulled one out and began to gently put her other things into it—her toothbrush and other toiletries.

"Julie, is it? What a common name. You know, you look familiar. Do I know your family?" Mrs. Waite couldn't have been more clear. She thought Julie was beneath her.

"I'm sure you do. I hear there are all sorts of slime balls that hang out in the sewage. Next time I see a snake in the grass, I'll think of you." Julie went to the kitchen door. "If you will excuse me, I'm leaving. Mrs. Waite, it was...different. Dr. Waite, you can rot in hell."

Julie turned and Cain grabbed her arm. Coming full around, she slammed her fist into his jaw. He fell back as she cried out in pain. Sudden and sharp pain throbbed in her fingers all the way to her elbow. Julie didn't move fast enough when out of the corner of her eye, she saw something flash toward her. Even a glancing blow hurt like hell. Julie staggered back quickly and caught the counter with her hand. When Mrs. Waite came at her a second time, the tea pot raised, Julie just managed to get out of the way before the pot hit the tile counter, breaking three of the pretty white tiles. Mrs. Waite drew back again.

"That's enough," roared Cain. Everyone froze as his voice echoed through the large kitchen.

"She started it," Mrs. Waite sobbed. "And she hurt my poor Roscoe too. She's just an upstart. She's just trying to get at your money. She wants to...oh, please tell me you aren't fucking her!"

Cain didn't answer.

Julie could feel the blood running down the side of her head and her hand was throbbing like a bad tooth. She didn't wait for Cain to decide what he was going to tell his mother, but went to the door and out of it. She didn't run, but she didn't walk either. She was about a mile down the road when a horn blaring behind her made her turn around.

"Get in," Quinn ordered. "I told him I'd take you to the hospital. I promise I won't ask questions, but I will see that you're helped."

Julie didn't even know where she was. Staring down at the woman in the driver's seat, Julie wanted to ask her why. She didn't know what for, but she did.

"I'm very pissed at Cain myself right now. I promise you I won't take you back there. Hell, if I had somewhere else to go, I would too. I just want to make sure that you're all right. I just need to make sure my mother didn't hurt you too badly. Please, Julie."

Julie nodded, walked around to the passenger side of the car, and got in. Dizziness rolled through her like a freight train. She didn't lower her head like she wanted to, but did lean it against the cool glass at the door.

"There's a free clinic on Hudson Avenue. Is that far from where we are?" When Quinn shook her head no, Julie continued. "Could you please just drop me off there? I'll be fine there."

"I'll wait for you," Quinn said.

They drove for another five minutes when Julie remembered her borrowed clothes.

"Keep them. I'm not sure what's going on between you and my brother, but he shouldn't have said that about you. Especially not to her. She's a vicious bitch and will never look at you with anything but disdain from now on."

Julie didn't care. She hoped she'd never see her again anyway. She didn't say anything and the rest of the ride was made in silence.

~~~

Cain tried to call Quinn's cell phone number again and got the same thing, "cannot be reached at this time." He'd already called the hospital four times and after finding out that Julie hadn't been seen, he'd had Quinn paged. Still nothing. He was about to go out himself when his phone rang. It was Quinn.

"Where the fuck are you two? I've been trying to reach you for over three hours. Damn it, Quinn...are you all right?"

"Yes. I'm at the gate. You might as well know now that Julie isn't with me. So if you want to turn me away, now would be as good a time as any," she told him.

Cain wanted to scream at her, rant and rave too, but he simply pressed the button to allow her inside the boundaries. How could she think that he'd turn her away? Why would she think he'd do something like that? He knew why. He'd been an ass to Julie, a bastard to her really.

As soon as he heard her car door shut, he met her at the back door from the kitchen. She looked exhausted and there was a glazed, pained look in her eyes. He pulled her into his arms and held her. And when she finally put her arms around his waist and held him back, his heart leapt with joy.

"I'm so sorry, baby. So very sorry. Did you have someone look at your head too? If not, will you please allow me to look at it? I can see that you're in pain."

Cain wanted to ask about Julie, but he knew that if he pushed his sister, she'd not tell him anything. When she nodded, he sat her in a kitchen chair and went to get his bag. Jazzie was in the living room and followed him into the kitchen. Cain began examining Quinn while Jazzie made some tea.

"Julie is at the women's shelter, though I don't know why. She is the most stubborn woman I've ever...they treat people like shit down there. I was surprised they even put the ten stitches in her head. *Ouch!* Watch it, that hurt."

Anger again at his mother had him pressing too hard on the wound at her head. The fact that his mother had been so pissed that Quinn had "bothered" with the tramp and had gone on about her even after Cain had told her to shut up had him throw her out.

"I'm sorry." He forced himself to take a deep breath and to be more careful. "Are they keeping her overnight? Or is she back...back out on the streets again?"

Quinn stilled his hands and looked at him. "I didn't know she was homeless when I agreed to take her to the clinic. They gave her...no one should be treated that way, Cain. I don't care who you are or how little money you have. They wouldn't keep her. They called her a trouble maker and after they treated her, they practically threw her out." Quinn stood and hugged Cain again. "She's such a fighter. And Mother...I think I hate her and Father more...Cain, they've been so...oh, Cain." Her sobbing tore through him. And when he felt Jazzie come up beside him, he pulled her into his embrace as well.

Cain held his sisters while they cried. He wanted to join them, but knew that he couldn't. He also knew that he had to find her, find Julie and care for her.

"Like I said, she's at the women's shelter on Tenth. They've seen her before and took her in even though they didn't have any room. They told her she could sleep on the couch in the rec room until morning." Quinn backed up and dug something out of her pocket. "I gave them your number in case something happens. I also gave her one of these. She thinks it was an aspirin. Something else you should know, I really like her."

Cain looked down at the small brown bottle. It took him several seconds to realize what it was. Codeine. He raised a brow at her. His sister had slipped Julie a Micky.

"I like her too, Cain. What are you going to do about her?" Jazzie asked as she sat down with three mugs of hot tea.

"I fucked up with her. Badly. But I want to fix it."

Before he could say more, his phone rang. The number was one he'd never seen before.

"That'll be the shelter. They'll need you to show some sort of identification to get her, but they can't help you with her if she wakes up. Oh, and you are going to volunteer your services there twice a month. As a goodwill gesture."

Cain stared at Quinn for a full minute before it registered what she was saying. Jazzie's "get the hell out of here" had him racing to the door. He turned quickly and hugged them both again before going to his car. He was bringing her home.

~CHAPTER TEN~

Julie woke slowly. She didn't have a clue where she was or how she had gotten there. Rolling to her side, she looked at the sleeping nurse sitting in the chair. Julie looked around the room and saw that while furnished, there didn't seem to be anything personal around, just like she'd seen at Cain's house. One thing she was certain of, she wasn't in the shelter.

The furniture was old, but not worn. There were several antiques spread around the room mixed in with the newer pieces, a rocker and stool where the nurse now sat. Julie had seen the same set in her mother's home, but smaller and back in the servants' rooms. A coat rack and a beautiful lamp were in the corner. The bed she was in was a simple full-sized bed. The two dressers were nice, but like the rest of the room, devoid of pictures or small things that made the room look like anyone lived in it.

There was a braided rug under the chair the nurse was sitting in. The room was too dark to tell what the colors were, but Julie thought there were deep reds and dark blues.

Knowing that she had somehow ended up in someone's house, Julie had a good idea whose it might be. She moved the blankets back and started to sit up. Dizziness swamped her. She thought she had moaned out loud, but either the nurse was a very heavy sleeper, or Julie had only thought she had.

It took Julie a few minutes to get to the side of the bed. That's when she realized she couldn't go without help. Hating to wake the other woman, Julie called out to her. The nurse woke immediately.

"Oh, miss, I'm so very sorry. I've been so busy of late. What, this place was is dusty bunny's haven, it was." The nurse hopped up and began to help Julie. "I'm Dottie Webb, I am. My, you are beaten up, aren't you? Come on, love, let's get you to the bath, shall we?"

Julie barely noticed the accent she was in so much pain. She wanted to scream. Every part of her body hurt, not just hurt, but pounded pain at her. She tried to keep any moans to herself, but it was just too much. She'd been beaten more times in the past few days than she'd been in most of her adult life.

"Please. Please, I beg you, I can't move just yet. Just leave me here and go out and find a gun. It will be a mercy killing, I swear to you. You won't go to jail. I'll leave them a note for you."

Mrs. Webb looked horrified. Julie was only about half kidding. But when she left Julie, she thought maybe she was going to put her out of her misery. Tears streamed down her face. She was in so much pain, so when the nurse returned empty-handed, Julie couldn't help it, she sobbed.

"You don't be moving from there, child. I've called the troops, I have. Someone will be here just shortly to see you though," Mrs. Webb said with a look of determination on her face.

"I think you should just shoot me. I know I'd feel better in the long run. I know I'd feel a damned sight better than I do right now." When Mrs. Webb only tisked at her, Julie continued. "I don't suppose you can tell me where I am, could you? I know this is someone's home. Is it yours?"

"'Tis Dr. Cain Waite's home you'd be in. He called me just yesterday. Retired, I was, but he was looking for some extra help and I some extra monies. Do you want to try and stand now, miss? You don't look so pale now."

Julie knew that was where she was, but the reality of the situation was still a bit of a shock. Moving to the edge of the bed more, she stood up, the need to leave overriding the pain that riddled her. But the need was overpowered by the tilting room and the belly lurch. Julie reached out and grabbed the first thing she touched.

"Come on," the voice said in a strained way. "Let's get you back to bed. Damn it, Julie, do you have to make everything so difficult?"

Julie looked up into the stormy eyes of Cain. "Fuck you. I didn't ask you to bring me...how the hell did you bring me here, come to think of it? Never mind. I'm leaving. I just have to pee, let me go."

Julie tried pulling away, but the next thing she knew, he was scooping her up into his arms and taking her into the bathroom. She tried in vain to pull the t-shirt, which she just noticed wasn't hers and was huge on her, down to a modest cover up.

"Put me down this instant! The nerve!" She tried to struggle out of his arms, but she was just hurting herself more.

"Shut up. I swear...here. I'll stand right out here and you do your business. And be careful. You don't need any more bruises on you."

Glaring up at him, Julie wanted to cry. Damn him. He had no right to be pissy with her. She was a grown woman, damn it.

"I can't...you have to leave. I can't pee with you standing there." She didn't think he would. She thought he would be just stubborn enough to stand right there until her body had done what he wanted.

"I'll be right outside the room. If I hear one noise, one sound that I don't like, I swear to you that I'm busting down this door and coming in. You hear me?" Cain roared at her.

"The fucking house can hear you, oh loud one. Like I give two shits if you bust down your own door." She moved toward the commode. "Out, and when I'm finished, I'm leaving here. You aren't my keeper. Nor are you my father, though there are times...get out!"

Cain mumbled something. She was sure as she was standing there that she didn't want to know, but he left her. She turned on the water tap full blast to drown out any sounds she might make and sat down to pee. But not before sticking her tongue out at the man on the other side of the door.

Julie started crying in earnest. While she didn't hurt as badly now—the moving around had loosened muscles—she did know without a doubt Cain wouldn't be letting her leave like she wanted. To be honest, she wasn't sure she'd get very far like this. Her head was pounding like a jackhammer had moved in. When she flushed and stood up, the room titled dangerously. She was afraid for all her bravado, she was going to fall and hit her poor head again.

Turning off the water, Julie could hear Cain talking to someone. When she opened the door, she noticed that he was still on his phone and Mrs. Webb was gone. Julie made her way back to the bed, but didn't sit down.

Reaching for her shoes with her feet, she ignored Cain. She felt that was the best way to win an argument with him. She began working her shoe onto her foot as he spoke.

"This is a house separate from the main house. I won't...you can stay here for as long as you want. No one...I won't bother you."

"I don't want anything from you, including this house. I was doing just fine until you stepped into my life and tried to take it over. Are you this bossy with everyone?"

"Yes."

She looked at him sharply. She could almost hear humor in his voice, but didn't know him that well. He looked like a man who didn't find humor in much. Then he continued and she wanted to bash his head in again.

"You do remember why I stepped into your life, don't you? You were lying in a pool of your own blood. I couldn't do anything but help you."

"I want to leave. I don't...you just don't understand. There are things going on that you couldn't understand." There are things going on that even she didn't understand, but didn't think he'd appreciate her knowing that.

Cain started pacing. He looked like a caged lion, all muscles and long limbs. When he stopped sharply and turned to her, she just knew that she wasn't going to like whatever it was he'd thought of. "You could be carrying my child. I don't want it to be born in a box somewhere. And before you get pissed again, Quinn told me you can't go back to the clinic. What happens if you're pregnant, Julie? Would you want to raise a baby like you currently live?"

Julie turned her back to him. Yes, she thought, what if? A baby would make things more...well, more everything. Not to mention it would be unsafe for them both. And she wasn't stupid, no matter what this man thought of her. She knew she had no choice. She had to stay. "I'll stay until I know for sure about your kid. But you need to stay away from me. You aren't my boss and I don't need you seeing after me. The nurse, Mrs. Webb, she doesn't have to watch me. I gave you my word. I don't need a sitter."

"No, Julie. I'm your doctor. And like it or not, I owe you. I'll see you once a day until you're healed. Then when the time is right, I'll take you somewhere and we'll have a pregnancy test performed. And Mrs. Webb is staying. She needs a place to stay as much as you do. She'll make sure you're eating right and taking care."

Julie continued to stare out the window, anywhere but at him. She knew that if she really wanted to, she could leave. But he was right. If there was a child, she couldn't carry it and raise it on the streets. She was too sore right now to even think about protecting herself, much less a child.

Without turning back to him, she nodded. She waited for him to say more, to say anything, but after about a minute, he simply left the room. Moving across the room to the window seat, Julie sat on it gingerly and stared unseeing out into the night. She wondered how long it would take to figure out if she was pregnant or not.

~~~

Cain went into the kitchen to find Mrs. Webb. He wanted to leave the house and scream and howl at the moon. But he knew that he needed to thank the elderly nurse first. She stood when he entered the room.

"The little miss, is she all right, Dr. Waite? The poor mite, looked all done in, she did. I hope you gave her something for the pain."

Pain. Cain had been so pissed at her he'd forgotten to ask if she wanted anything for pain. He doubted that she'd admit to him that she was in pain, but he still should have asked.

"No, I didn't...she is...she and I, we fight more than we talk. I'll leave you something if you could please see that she gets it for me. I'd be very grateful."

"Of course, sir. 'Twill be a pleasure. I know you said she was hurt and that she needed tending, but well, sir, if you don't mind me asking, why don't you have her with you? You being in love with her and all."

Cain looked at Mrs. Webb. In love? With Julie? He didn't think so. She was, why, most of the time he wanted to strangle her, but love her? No, that couldn't be right.

Cain was back at the main house before he realized it. He couldn't remember if he answered Mrs. Webb or even left her anything for Julie's pain. He couldn't even remember walking across the driveway and coming to his room. He was staring out into the night when he realized that he thought maybe he just might love the little twit. Now he had to figure out what the hell to do about it.

Looking at the bedside clock when his phone rang, he nearly didn't answer the private number. His family and a few friends were the only ones who had it. Coming to realize what his feelings for Julie were had him doubting his own sanity. So when he barked his name into the phone, he couldn't help but flush when laughter greeted his rudeness.

"It has to be a woman to have you sounding like a bear with his foot in a trap. They do that to you so often you check your feet regularly to see if you still have two. I'm assuming it's a woman because you're the only man I know that has five of the most beautiful sisters ever created and still doesn't have a clue."

Cain decided that the next time he saw Damon Grant, he was going to knock the older man on his flipping ass. "If you just called to be a pain in my ass then I have others here that are more than willing to do that. It's two in the morning, Damon, what the fuck do you want?"

Damon's laughter didn't improve his mood. Cain nearly hung up on the man. He didn't need this right now.

"Oh, Cain, I want so much. But I digress. I want you to come and be my partner at the office. I had to wait until your forms came through, impressive by the way, and your transcripts. First in your class at med school, class president, the list is as long as it is impressive. What do you say?"

Cain felt behind him for the chair and sat even though he hadn't found it. The floor hit his ass hard. It was cold and unforgiving, but he didn't feel a thing.

"You want me to come and work for you? In your practice?" Cain heard the squeak in his voice and was grateful when Damon didn't mention it.

"No. I want you to be my partner—as equals. I know you just got bought out by the other firm in Maine. Too bad about that. But they only had good things to say about you. Phillip said you'd make a great partner and told me that I'd be a stupid man to let you go. And we both know that I'm not a stupid man."

Cain tried in vain to wrap his head around what Damon was saying to him. He and his partners had parted on good terms. They wanted to go in a more modern way of seeing patients, stacking them three deep so they could see more patients in less time. Cain preferred the old ways, seeing each patient for as long as they wanted or even needed. He didn't think the other way was going to save them any money in the long run.

"No. No, you're not stupid. Why? I mean, why me and why now?" Cain thought about his sister. "Quinn put you up to this, didn't she? I'm going to pound her ass but good when I find her." Cain could hear Damon's laughter again.

"Ah, Cain my boy, you always were a distrusting sort of young man. Not that I blame you. You didn't have much reason at all to trust, did you? But no, this is a legitimate offer I'm giving you. I'd genuinely like for you to become my partner."

Cain had always dreamed of becoming Damon's partner, his equal, ever since he'd set his leg as a teenager. Damon had been beyond kind to the younger Cain, making sure that Cain had had his pain under control and managed before he'd let him go. And when Cain had started crying when the pain became overwhelming, Damon had simply let him, not saying anything neither then nor now.

"Yes. I would be honored to work with you. You have...I can't believe this. Thank you, Damon. I won't let you down."

"I know you won't, son. Come by the office tomorrow around noon. We'll go and get some lunch and iron out the details. Devin will be my attorney, of course, and if you trust him, he can finalize the paperwork for us as soon as possible. I'm happy to have you aboard."

After they hung up, Cain sat on the floor for several minutes before he jumped up and went down the stairs. He wanted to tell Julie. No, he needed to tell her. Going into the kitchen, there she stood with her shirt in her hands and his t-shirt on her body.

~*CHAPTER ELEVEN*~

Julie looked at Cain. She had only just come in the door, needed to use his washer to clean her only other pair of pants and shirts. She started to back toward the door again. "I didn't mean to wake you. There isn't any washer next door and I needed to get these...I should leave." She back closer to the door and was nearly there when he moved.

"No."

That single word made her heart race and her blood heat and rush through her body. It hadn't sounded so much like a command as it did a plea. She pulled her clothes closer to her and moved two steps back from his body, now trapping her against the counter.

"I was just coming to see you." Now his voice was soft and rough.

Need rippled through her body. Sharp and hot. When he gently ran is fingers down her injured cheek, she had to close her eyes against the overwhelming feelings that raced over and through her.

"I thought you'd be." She had to swallow hard to continue. "I thought you'd be asleep by now."

"No. Julie, I want you." His voice was just a whisper of a sound, a breath away from her mouth. She could see him leaning closer to her, his hand gently cupping the back of her head and bringing her forward.

"We can't do this," she heard herself say as she licked her suddenly dry lips. Her body wasn't listening to her. Her hands moved up his chest and to his neck without her permission. When his mouth was close enough that she could feel his hot breath on her lips, she knew she was lost, knew that he was going to make love to her again. And she just couldn't make herself pull away from him.

Cain's mouth covered hers, gently brushing hers the first time, then the second brush a little firmer. When he passed over her the third time, he ran his tongue along her moistened lips and groaned. Even as he slanted his mouth fully over hers, she knew that she was lost.

Julie felt him savor her, his mouth almost worshipped in his tenderness. But her body needed his now, needed his with an urgency that nearly consumed her. She was afraid. Afraid of him and what he would mean, what it would mean for them to become lovers.

"Cain, please, we can't..."

When Cain lifted her by her ass and sat her onto the counter behind her, she wrapped her legs around him, his fullness and hardness pressed against her. She suddenly became aware of her near naked state. Pressing her closer, she realized he knew it too. Cain buried his cock into her soft folds, leaving her no doubt that his needs were as sharp as hers.

As he rocked into her, her groan slipped from her mouth. When he lifted her again, she instinctively wrapped her legs tighter around him, pulling him closer, his mouth never leaving hers. He was moving her toward the stairs, up to his room. She needed to try just one more time.

"We can't do this. You don't even like me," she growled at him, her voice husky and soft.

"If you don't want me as badly as I do you, then say so. That's the only way that I'm stopping now. The only way you're going to get me to put you down and walk away." He stared at her, waiting.

Julie couldn't do it. She knew that she couldn't walk away, nor could she let him. Leaning back into his mouth, she wrapped her hands deep into his hair and put all that she could into her kiss. Her body rocked hard into his even as she knew she was making a mistake. But she needed him.

Suddenly, they were in his bedroom again. He lowered her to his bed and he followed her down. When her back touched the bed, he reached between them and began working at the buttons down the front of the shirt she had on. Finally, in obvious frustration, he ripped it open and buttons scattered everywhere.

"Christ, but you're beautiful."

His voice was silk and satin, his mouth wet and hot as he lowered it to her breast. As soon as his tongue flicked over her, Julie arched up to demand more. As he took her nipple into his mouth, Julie nearly screamed out, her body on fire with need.

"Please, Cain. Please, I need you." His chuckle nearly had her scream at him. If she thought she wouldn't die of need, she'd get up and leave his laughing ass to fend for himself. Running her fingers through his hair, she jerked his head up from her nipple and nearly groaned again from the loss. "If you aren't inside of me very soon, I'm going to kick your ass. You started this, now take me."

Cain's smile was sin. She knew in that moment that he was going to make her suffer, make her wait for him, and she would hurt before he finished. Her belly curled in anticipation, even her pussy, wet and swollen, seemed to gush more cream, swell more beneath his smile.

"I won't be rushed, love. I want to taste you, every single inch of you. I want to savor your nipples, lick your clit, and drink from you. I want to touch you deep, stretch you for me while I fuck you with my tongue. Then when

I've made sure you're ready, I'm going to slam my cock deep into your hot, wet pussy and fuck you slow. I want to feel you tighten around me, feel the slick, hot walls of you pull and milk me. Don't rush me, Julie, or I'll slow down even more."

As Cain lowered his head again to her breast, she knew without a doubt he would do as he said. He would drive her near the edge and not let her fall. When Cain bit her nipple just this side of pain then licked the tiny hurt, Julie knew she was in trouble.

"Are you in any pain?" Cain asked her. As if he only just realized that she had been hurting before, not an hour ago. To be honest, she'd forgotten all about the pain when he'd touched her.

"No. Well, not really. You...are you going to stop and not have sex with me?" Her voice sounded like she felt— soft, sexy, hot. She also knew that she would kill him if he said no.

"No. I'm not having sex with you, Julie. I want to make love to you, with you. But if you tell me no for real, I will stop."

Yeah, she thought, *and I'll die too*. He was sure she was going to tell him no, to turn him away. She also knew he would never force her, never in a million years, but there was a need inside of her like a living, breathing flame. He waited for her to speak, to tell him she wanted him to take her. When she didn't answer right away, he sat up on his knees and looked down at her. She hadn't answered him so he ran his fingers gently up her thigh and toward the triangle of tight curls just over her sex that she was very sure were glistening wet.

Scooting back more, he ran his fingers along them then gently pressed his fingers into her wet heat. When her eyes fluttered close, he pulled out then back into her again and again.

"You're so wet," he moaned. "My fingers slide into your heat so easily. I'm going to taste you, fuck you with my tongue and fingers until you come in my mouth."

Moving down her body so that he was inches from doing just what he'd said he would she sat up just enough to watch him through hooded eyes. She looked down her body at him, watched as he lowered his head. When he spread her open enough with his fingers, Cain licked her from gate to clit.

Even as he tasted her, Julie fought against her need for him. Cain's tongue moved along her clit and then he suckled it into his mouth as his fingers moved into her again and again. She could feel her pussy tighten around him, gushing cream, her need into his waiting mouth. Without her realizing it, Julie wrapped her leg over his shoulder, first one then the other, until she was riding his mouth and fingers with wild abandonment.

"Come, Julie," he told her huskily. "Come in my mouth. Let me taste you, all of you."

She tried to fight against the overwhelming need to do just what he'd commanded. She tried pulling back, pulling away from him, tried thinking about anything but the delicious things he was doing to her body. When he hit the spot inside of her, the sweet spot that she craved him to stroke, she bit her lip so hard she tasted blood. When he began to slow his movements, his tongue and his fingers, she was nearly crying with relief until he pulled her clit into his mouth and pressed his fingers around her tight rosette.

Julie tried to pull away, her body fighting her all the way, knowing that if he did what she thought he was going to do, she'd never be able to hang on. Just as that thought entered her head, he pressed his finger deep into her.

She screamed as her climax ripped through her. Every time he pressed deeper into her, her body surged again up and over the edge. Climax after climax slammed into her until she had no idea when one was ending and another was starting.

Cain moved then. His body moved up hers and she could feel his cock, hard and thick along her thigh as he reached above her head. Reaching out, she grabbed onto him, trying to pull his body to her, into hers. Need for him inside of her was paramount over everything else. When Cain pulled away, his body leaving hers, Julie felt it to her very core. The overwhelming stark loneliness made her whimper.

The sound of foil ripping had her looking up at him and her body responded again to see his hard cock as he rolled the condom over him. Moving back up her body, nipping and tasting her as he went, she felt every touch like he was marking her with a branding iron. When he took her mouth, marking it, claiming it at the same time his body did, entering her hard and fast, he stilled immediately. Her heart thundered in her chest.

"Please...please, I need...fuck me, Cain. Please, fuck me," she begged.

"You'll come to me. Every night as long as you live next door to me, you'll let me fill you, fuck you, Julie. Every night."

Cain slimmed deep into her, stretching her, filling her, stroke after stroke until he exploded into her, bringing her with him into an earth-shattering climax.

He dropped heavily onto her. Julie may have thought him too heavy, but she couldn't move, couldn't speak. When Cain rolled to his back, taking her with him, she laid her head on his pounding heart and closed her eyes against the pain.

He wanted her in his bed, but not his home. Not only that, but she would do so willingly. Julie dared not move as she laid there, her heart broken at what she'd done. She'd just become Cain's whore.

When his breathing evened out and his heartbeat gentled under her cheek, Julie waited until the hall clock chimed once for the four o'clock hour then again for the five o'clock hour before she moved. When he simply rolled to his side, she slipped out of the bed.

For long moments, she stared down at him. His face was so relaxed in slumber. He looked so young and carefree. Julie found herself wanting to brush the hair from his forehead, the curls that fought for control, but she didn't dare wake him. He'd been clear on her boundaries. Pulling her tattered shirt around her, she went to his door, opened it slightly, and slipped into the empty hall. Moving down the stairs, Julie picked up her shirt and other clothing she'd brought to wash into her arms and went blindly into the night, tears flooding her eyes.

Once in the small cottage, Julie washed her shirt and the two pair of panties in the sink in the bathroom, wringing them out as best she could. She hung them over the shower curtain. Finding a fan in the closet, she took it into the bathroom, set it to blow over her clothes, and went back to the window seat. Staring out into the dark night sky, Julie thought about what had brought her to his point. The reason she had run, had become nothing in the first place. Her family.

Julie's father and her very best friend had died of a sudden heat attack two weeks before. Still reeling and in so much pain and shock, she had gone to dinner with her mother, Uncle Samuel, her father's brother, and her two brothers. They had just left the attorney's office after the reading of the will, leaving Julie the youngest and the richest woman in the world.

"I still can't believe he left you everything, Alyssa. And would you please stop looking like someone just took your last piece of cake? It's been a month. Get over it and move on," her mother snarled at her.

"It's been two weeks, not a month. And I will mourn how I please for as long as I please. If this is why you wanted me to meet you, then I have more important things to see to." She stood to leave.

Although Alyssa was only seventeen at the time, she'd not lived at home for more than three years. She'd been set up first in an apartment in the city with maids to "care" for her then as recently as six months ago, alone. Her father had seen how she and her mother had fought constantly and had made these arrangements to please them both, but mostly Alyssa. Shannon Howard did not like having her daughter around to remind her of her fading beauty and Alyssa didn't—no, wouldn't be the little girl her mother wanted. Alyssa didn't want to be in pageants like the other little girls; she wanted to go to school. Alyssa was top in her class everywhere she went, yet she forbade the papers from telling her story. Things like pink rooms and frilly dresses made her ill; her hair and nails being done was not something she could sit still for, and meeting her mother for luncheons and teas with her friends was completely out of the question.

"Sit down," Shannon hissed at Alyssa, looking around the restaurant. "My God, is everything a battle with you? Sit down, Alyssa, or so help me, I will never speak to you again."

Alyssa smiled. She knew it was an empty threat. According to the will, Shannon would need to speak to her daughter if she wanted to continue to live in the manner her father had decreed in his will. Alyssa even owned the house she was staying in, lock, stock, and barrel, as her daddy used to say. Apparently, her daddy had known about the affairs his wife had been having right under his nose. And he had gone to great lengths to ensure that Shannon knew it as well. Julie could almost hear her daddy laughing at what he'd done.

Alyssa sat. Not because she had to, but because she wanted to hear what she had to say to her.

"You have five minutes. Then I'm going home. Spill it or not, Mother. I could care less what you think you might have to say to me that I might find important."

"All right." Shannon looked around the table. "I'm not going to let you ruin my life again, Alyssa. I've had enough of your—"

"Me ruin yours?" Alyssa asked incredulously. "How on earth do you figure I had anything to do with the way you fucked up your life? Could it be one of the tens of dozens of men you fucked in Daddy's bed, or maybe the fact that these two"—she pointed at her brothers—"aren't even his?"

That was another revelation that came out at the reading. Just Alyssa was her father's child. The boys, Nathan and Robert, were from two different men before Alyssa had even been born.

"You'll be married soon enough and you'll see how hard it is to remain faithful to just one man. But that's your problem, not mine." Shannon glanced at her brother-in-law, Samuel. "The reason I've asked you here it to tell you that you'll be marrying your uncle sometime next week. He needs a child because of your father's idiotic will and you are...breedable. Samuel will let you have his child."

Alyssa looked at her mother in amazement. Then at her uncle Samuel, who was licking his lips and leering at her. Alyssa couldn't stop the sudden disgust that went through her body.

"No and hell no. Have his...you do realize that he's my uncle, right? And that beyond that being the sickest thing that I've ever heard, it's also very dangerous. It's not going to happen anyway." Alyssa felt her belly roll and then her head start to swim. She looked down at the tea glass that had been there when she sat down. Then at her mother. Alyssa thought she had only had one sip, but she'd been so mad she couldn't remember.

"Yes, Alyssa, I drugged you. I can see that it's starting to take its affect on you. I knew you wouldn't cooperate so I had to take matters into my own hands."

Alyssa stood and staggered.

"It won't matter if you try to get away. You'll be down before you know it and he'll have you tonight or tomorrow." Her mother stood too.

"Stay away...stay..." The room began to spiral and she knew that if she fell, they'd be on her like a pack of hungry wolves. Moving toward the bathroom, Alyssa fell into a waitress and asked where a bathroom was. When she pointed in the opposite direction, Alyssa stuck her finger down her throat and threw up. She felt bad for the poor waitress who had gotten most of it, but it did give Alyssa what she needed. A diversion and a semi-empty belly. She slipped out the kitchen door and to a man in a box that would protect her for years.

~CHAPTER TWELVE~

Cain woke at eleven. He looked at his cell phone and remembered his appointment with Damon. Rushing out of the bed and into the shower, he wondered about Julie. When he'd gone into the bathroom to shower, the condom was still on and he flushed with need again. He'd hoped that she'd still be in bed with him when he woke and was disappointed when she wasn't. He smiled when he thought about her moving in with him.

Cain was rushing down the stairs when he saw Quinn and Jazzie at the kitchen table. He needed them to help him out and thought of the best way to get their help. Grabbing a glass from the cabinet and pouring some tea from the refrigerator, he turned to look at them. "I was wondering if one of you could run Julie into town today? I have to go in to meet Damon for something and I don't know how long I'll be. She needs some—"

"I'm not leaving her there. She can stay with me in my room if I have to. I'll not leave her like that again, Cain, and you can't make me," Quinn said as she stood up.

"I don't want you to lea...Christ, Quinn, I want her to move in with me. I don't want her on the streets anymore than you do. She is...I mean, I don't want...shit. She needs some clothes and I thought that...you know, just forget it. I'll take her later." He turned away. He didn't know why that had hurt him, them thinking he was taking her back to the streets, but it did.

"I'm sorry, Cain. I truly am. I just...I really like her and she seems so...do you think she's running from someone or something? I want her safe either way," Quinn said as she laid her head on his chest.

Cain gathered her closer in his arms. Quinn had been married before. Carl Wickett was an abusive prick that had knocked Quinn around whenever something didn't set well with him, which usually meant anything and everything that he could think of. His sister Sin had taken Quinn and Jazzie to a self-defense class every day when Carl had been in the hospital for something else. When he'd come home mean and abusive, he'd never expected his wife to fight back, or to be so good at it.

After Carl had spent five days in the hospital and another month in physical therapy, he'd left town and had not returned since. When Quinn had received her divorce papers the next week, she'd signed them and returned them the same day. Carl Wickett hadn't made a visit since.

"Are you paying for this shopping spree? If so, I want to go too. I think our little Julie could use our advice on shopping and buying, especially with someone else's money. She should spend some time with us anyway before you pop the question. That way we can charm her into saying yes for you." Quinn looked up at Cain when he didn't answer.

"Are you going to marry Julie, Cain? That's wonderful. I want to plan it for you. I bet the gardens are beautiful here. I think in the garden by the pool. Oh, Cain, she'll make a wonderful bride, don't you think?" Jazzie asked as she came to him for her share of the hug.

"Let me ask her first, all right? Then I should...I don't know who she's hiding from or why. She could be some long lost heiress hiding from her evil family for all I know." They all laughed.

He kissed both his sisters and left the house. He knew they'd get Julie what she needed whether she wanted it or not. He grinned to himself about that wishing he could be there when that conversation took place.

Cain was five minutes late for his appointment, but it wasn't bad. Damon had an emergency and he himself was running behind as well. At twelve-forty they were just sitting down to a nice lunch at one of Cain's and Damon's favorite restaurants, Muddy Misers. It was a nice mid-priced place with great food and great service. Devin joined the men at a little after one in the afternoon.

~~~

"I'm pretty sure Cain meant for us to go shopping at a nice store. Like in the mall across town. Not that there isn't...you can't be serious, Jaz, that color is hideous!" Quinn was ready to strangle them both.

They had left the house as soon as they'd found Julie sitting in the kitchen talking with Mrs. Webb. Julie had balked at first, not wanting to go out. Quinn could tell she was still sore and she moved a little slowly when she first got up, but she finally said yes. They were out the door in ten minutes.

"This is a store and I do believe we are shopping. Though you don't seem to be buying anything. I thought you said you were going to make your brother buy you some nice summer clothes? Besides, it's Tuesday...oh, Jazzie, Quinn is right, that color puce just isn't right for you. Why don't you try this nice lemony color on? I think it will suit your hair color much better," Julie said as she dug through a pile of shirts.

Quinn watched the woman in the dark green pants eyeing their purses again. She'd been following them around since they came in and she didn't look as if she worked there. Quinn pulled the cart holding their purses and a pile of clothes closer to her as she turned back to Julie again.

"What I think he meant was for us to...wait! What does Tuesday have to do with why we're shopping at Goodwill?" Quinn wasn't even sure she wanted to know.

"Everything is half price today," Julie said to her, as if that explained everything. Then Julie leaned closer to her. "Quinn, she doesn't want your purse. She wants you. That's Lily, she likes women."

Quinn looked sharply at Julie as she moved to the next rack of shirts. She wasn't sure if she was kidding or not then she looked back at the woman Julie had called Lily. She winked at Quinn.

"I'm sorry. I don't...I'm with them," Quinn pointed at her sister and Julie. "Not with them, with them, but...we're related. All of...the blond is my sister and...and I...I'm sorry, I don't swing that way." She felt stupid and embarrassed.

Lily smiled at Quinn as if knowing she was flustered. "It don't hurt none to look, do it? You're a fine woman. If you change your mind, have Sally there..." She pointed at Julie. "Have her contact me. I can make you forget everything."

Lily blew her a kiss and left the store. It took Quinn a full minute to realize that she had just been propositioned. She wasn't sure whether to be insulted or flattered. She turned back to the other two.

Quinn tried to rush them along, wanting to put as much distance between her and Lily as she could, but soon realized it was not going to happen. They were having too much fun. Julie wasn't doing as much shopping, Quinn noticed, as she was herding Jazzie. Jazzie simply had the worst taste in clothes and Quinn wondered why she hadn't noticed it before. Julie was also careful of the things that they bought, watching zippers and buttons, making sure that there were no stains on things that couldn't be easily removed. And when Jazzie had wanted to try things on, it was Julie who told her to leave her clothes on and try them on at home after she washed them. Quinn tried not to think about the reason for that bit of advice.

At the checkout, Quinn was impressed. Jazzie had spent eight dollars and twelve cents and had nine small bags stuffed full of shirts and pants that would look good on her. And Julie had one and has spent a dollar seven. Cain was going to be pissed about it too. Not that he was a snob, but that Julie had purchased her own things. With a pocket full of change no less.

At four forty-five, having gotten lunch and some things at Wal-Mart, the women were about to get into the car when Quinn's phone rang. She didn't want to answer it and nearly didn't. Groaning at the woman, she answered. "What is it, Mother? I'm busy and I don't have time for your shit today. Say what you want then leave me alone."

"What a way to speak to me, Quinn. I'm your mother. You should have more respect for me than you do. I did bring you into this world."

"Yes, you did. It is the only thing you've done for me that I'm grateful for. Time is wasting, Mother, what do you want?" Quinn hated her mother and wished every day that she could just be like Cain and tell her to fuck off.

"Can you and Jazzie come and get me? My car broke down and I can't get in touch with your brother at that restaurant. They won't give him a message. Please? Leave that woman on the street. She's belongs there anyway."

Quinn stilled. Leave Julie on the street, she'd said. Quinn looked around the parking area and realized they were very much alone. That's when she noticed the car, a dark sedan coming toward them.

"Get in the car. Now!"

Neither woman asked anything but scrambled to do what she had demanded. Quinn tried to hurry, but they were making mistakes, big ones, in trying to get in. It didn't matter anyway. The men jumped out of the car and rushed them before she got the car into drive.

The window on the passenger side exploded inward, spraying Jazzie with glass. Before Quinn could get the car moving, her side window exploded too. Glass cut into her skin and she felt it tear into her. The man grabbed at her hand as she tried to reach for the shifter and put the car into drive. The sound of the rear door window breaking registered a second before Jazzie started screaming. One man was choking Jazzie and trying to put his hand over her mouth. Another man was doing the same to Quinn. She could hear Julie in the back shouting too, but it was if sound had become muted and everything had slowed down. She was dying, she thought. This man was going to kill her and her mother was involved.

Quinn felt the car lurch and the guy with his hands around her throat let go for just a second. Moving Jazzie's foot off the steering column, Quinn put the car into drive and slammed her foot onto the gas. She heard a sickening thud-thud, but didn't even stop to think what she might have hit and kept going.

Quinn's throat hurt. She couldn't swallow, nor could she take a very deep breath. Blood smeared across her arms as she drove and she could feel a cut in her head bleeding down her neck. She didn't look at the women in the car with her. She was afraid if she did, she might give into the hysteria that was pushing in on her and scream bloody murder. The only thing she did was concentrate on driving, stopping at lights, and going with the traffic. Her single thought was, "hospital, hospital, hospital."

Quinn would never be sure how she made it to the hospital. Nor would she be sure how they made it inside before she fell apart. She could hear Julie saying something, talking to the nurses as she led her to the back room. Quinn heard, "shock," and, "head injury." At one point, she heard her say something about Cain, but thought that was a bad idea. He would be angry with her. She'd wrecked his car.

"I don't think he'll care much, Quinn. You saved your sister's and your life. I think he'll be much happier about that." Quinn looked at Julie. She hadn't realized she'd said that out loud.

Julie was bleeding and there was a horrific bruise on her left cheek and around her throat too. When Quinn reached up to run her finger along it, Julie stepped back. Something flashed in her eyes, regret and something else, but was gone before Quinn could recognize it.

"Julie?"

"They're calling your brother. I'm not sure how long it will be before he gets here. The police have been called too. You saved us, Quinn. If nothing else, you remember that, all right?"

"You're leaving, aren't you? Julie, don't go. Please, we can fix whatever you're running from. Cain has money, we can fix this. He loves you."

Pain. It was pain that had flashed in Julie's eyes because it was there again. Before Quinn could ask about it, Julie started backing away.

"I have to leave. I'm sorry. You...you're wrong about Cain. He just wanted sex. I'm sorry."

Julie turned to leave out the side curtain just as a nurse came through the other side. Quinn started to get up and go after her, but the nurse pulled her back into the bed. Suddenly, Quinn couldn't hold her head upright and the room spun out of control.

~CHAPTER THIRTEEN~

Cain rushed into the emergency room. One of the desk nurses simply pointed him to the back area and he went around the corner of the desk without a word. He barely registered that there were police milling around and that Cait was there as well. He had a goal in mind and nothing was keeping him from it. Finding the correct curtained area on the first try, his knees nearly buckled when he saw Jazzie sitting on the bed with Quinn.

"We're all right, Cain. I swear. They have to stitch up my arms and Quinn has a concussion, but we're fine."

Cain could hear her speaking, but the words weren't registering. He seemed to be missing the part of his brain that could think for some reason. He did manage to sit down when a chair was shoved under him. After a few seconds, he could hear Damon talking to his sisters.

"...the reason that doctors can't see their family. You'd have them puking all over you and that would cause a serious infection. Let me have a look at that cut now, Quinny, darling."

Cain and Damon had been about to sign the contract when the police had called him. All he could get from them was that his car had been in an accident and that one man was dead. His heart had skipped several beats before Damon had taken the phone from him and motioned for Devin to pay the check. They were in the car and on their way before Cain realized it. Devin drove while Damon shouted things into his phone.

Cain stood and when he knew that his legs weren't going to collapse, he stepped to the bed and pulled Jazzie into his arms. He had to hold them, keep them to him. He looked around the room, but before he could ask, Jazzie spoke.

"She's not here. Julie, she's not here. I don't know what happened to her, but one minute she was directing everyone to take care of us, then she was gone. I've looked everywhere for her and just so you know, Cait Grant isn't happy about her leaving either."

"Cain, I'm going to have to stitch Quinn up. You want to step out or stick around? I think I remember how to do it."

Cain nodded at him. "I'll stay. I can't leave them just yet."

Cain knew that if anyone would understand him, it would be Damon. The Grant brothers were the closest family he'd ever seen and their wives blended into the family as though they had been meant to be there. He loved them as much as he did his own sisters. Cait came around the corner just as Damon was starting to close up the wound on his sister's head.

"Cain? Do you know where we might find Julie? I need to ask her a few questions. Some things...something has come up."

Cain didn't like the way she'd said that, as if something he really didn't want to know had been discovered. He didn't want to leave his family, but Cait was nodding toward the other side of the curtain and he felt that he really didn't have a choice in the matter.

The room Cait had led him to was already occupied with Devin. He didn't look any happier than he felt, but Cain didn't say anything.

"I need to tell you something, but it can't go any further than this room. Cain, how much do you know about Julie?"

Cain looked up at Cait. "Know? Nothing really. She's homeless and lives around or near the Howard Building on Broad Street. She's been staying at the cottage on the property." He put his forehead on the table. He nearly told them that he was in love with her, but didn't. Couldn't for some reason.

No one said anything for a long time and Cain looked up. Cait had taken one of the chairs and was looking at Devin. Neither of them was speaking, but plenty was being said. He knew whatever they knew, he wasn't going to like.

"She's married, isn't she? Some big, beefy asshole is looking for her and found her to...oh, Christ, he was killed, wasn't he? Today, Quinn killed her husband."

"You do have a vivid imagination, don't you? No, she's not married. And her name isn't Julie." Cait slid a file toward him. "The other two men at the scene today had this on one of them. They've both been arrested. Take a look."

It was a few pictures of his sisters and Julie. They had been taken recently because he could just make out the bruise on Julie's cheek. They had been taken just inside the gates at his house. Cait reached over and flipped them over. On the back were notes and names. On the back of the pictures of his sisters were "not this one," but on Julie's it said, "I want her alive. The others, you can do whatever you want."

Cain closed the file and looked up at Devin. "Are my sisters in trouble? Should I contact the others and let them know? I don't know how to reach Sin, but I can try."

Cait pulled out another file. "No. This isn't about them, but about the woman calling herself Julie. You're sisters just happened to be with her when those men struck. Cain, Julie's name is Alyssa Marie Howard. Does that name ring a bell with you?"

Cain started to shake his head when he stopped and glanced over at Cait. "The Howard Building. She stays near there. That's where I've found her twice now. Is she related to them?"

Cait looked at Devin again and this time, Devin spoke. He pulled the file Cait had put on the desk closer to him and opened it. He pushed a photo in front of him. "This is Alyssa right before she disappeared nine years ago. She had just buried her father, Nathan Howard, two weeks before. They were having dinner in the Four Seasons, she and her mother Shannon Howard, Alyssa's two brothers, Nathan and Robert, and Nathan senior's younger brother Samuel. We don't know what happened that night, but Alyssa got sick and had went to the ladies room and never returned. She was seventeen."

The girl was Julie, or Alyssa, he thought. The photo showed a much younger and more carefree girl than the one he knew. Her smile was radiant and went to her eyes that sparkled with what looked like mischief and mirth. The man standing next to her had to be her father. There could be no doubt about that. And he looked at her with such love that Cain could almost feel it. He pushed them back at Devin.

"So? She's a runaway, so what? I don't understand what that has to do with what happened to my sisters." Cain could hear the hardness in his voice. He didn't care. She was a runaway and whatever had happened to his sisters today was her fault.

"I don't think she's a runaway. I don't know why, but I believe that she is—"

Cain stood up, cutting Devin off. "I have to see to my sisters. If you find this girl." Cain looked down at the picture of Julie/ Alyssa. "Tell her I said thanks for nothing. She nearly got my family killed today because she couldn't tell anyone who she was." He left the little room and went to find where Quinn and Jazzie were. He was angry and wasn't really sure why, or for that matter, at who. He found the room that Quinn was in and made sure that Jazzie was with her before he stepped into the hall to make a call.

"Mrs. Webb, I don't suppose that Julie is there, is she?"

"No, sir. She's gone already. She left you a note and a bag, though. She said if you called that I was to read it to you. Would you like for me to?"

Did he? Not really. He was just glad she was gone. He told her that he would read it when he got home.

"All right, sir. She also told me to tell you something else. She said she was sorry about your sisters."

"Thanks, Mrs. Webb. I appreciate that. But it's a little too late for that." He assured her that Miss Quinn and Miss Jazzie were all right.

"You think Miss Julie will get some help for her injuries, Dr. Waite? She was bleeding pretty badly when she left here. I tried to tend to them, but she wouldn't see it."

"I'm sure she'll be fine, Mrs. Webb." He didn't want to think about her being hurt. He didn't want to think about her at all. "She seems to be able to get whatever she needs."

Cain walked back into Quinn's room after hanging up and sat in the chair. Quinn was sleeping and Jazzie was curled up next to her on the bed asleep as well. He didn't want to wake them so he left the lights off and turned off his phone.

~~~

Alyssa moved along the building looking for the cubby hole. She had checked on it so much the first year that she was sure she'd never forget where it was. When she finally found it, she nearly cried in relief. Pulling out the loose brick and reaching inside, she pulled out the plastic bag. It was dried and brittle with age and covered in dirt and dust. She sat down on the ground and pulled it to her chest.

She sobbed for what she had allowed to happen to Quinn and Jazzie. Neither of them had had anything to do with what had happened all those years ago. And especially nothing to do with the man that had been killed today. Standing up, she made her way back to the hospital to give Molly Rodney's things.

Alyssa could no longer hide from who she was. Now that the police were involved, she knew it would be only a matter of time before someone recognized her. Cait Grant was too smart for her to let this go. And if anyone would figure it out, it would be Cait.

Looking over at the Howard Building, Alyssa saw someone she never thought she'd see again. Thomas Miller, her father's secretary. Before she could think twice about it, she was on her way toward him. He looked up at her when she said his name.

"Hello, my dear. I see you've finally come home. If you would be so kind, I would take you somewhere where we can talk. I have a nice private place in mind."

Alyssa simply got into the limo that had pulled to a soft stop beside them. Thomas opened the door before the driver could get out and handed her in, taking the small bag from her as he did. Once she was inside, he handed it back to her and sat across from her.

"You knew where I was, didn't you? All this time...Rodney, he told you."

"Yes, Mr. Kincaid and I have been watching over you for some time now. He contacted me just a few days after your picture came out in the papers. He said that you'd been drugged and that he wasn't sure it was safe for you to be found. I agreed." Thomas reached over, took out a first aid kit, and slid onto the seat next to her. "He reported to me weekly unless you needed something. I didn't like it at first, but when things around the office started to change, I decided that he was correct in keeping you away."

Alyssa put her hand on Thomas' and looked at him. "You know that it's only a matter of time now, don't you? In a few days it will hit the paper that…why hasn't it ever…?" She looked at him sharply. "Why you sly old devil. You're the reason that I've never been declared dead. What have you been up to?"

Thomas had the good grace to blush. "We took your picture at times when you slept or when you were not aware. It was a challenge at times to set them up. We needed to have them think you were elsewhere. Miss, I believe you will need a physician. I will take you to my home and we will see about getting you mended. You will need your strength, I believe, in dealing with the goings on."

Alyssa thought that was an understatement and leaned back in the limo as it started out. She hoped that Jazzie and Quinn were all right and hoped that Cain would forgive her someday.

Before she knew it, Alyssa was across town and in a big brownstone. Her father's family doctor was on his way to the house and she was being pampered for the first time in almost a decade. And for all that, she had never been so depressed in all her life.

The house was one that Thomas had lived in since he'd started working for Howard Incorporated. And it had changed little over the years. There was a pool out back now that Alyssa had seen on her way in, and the staff was different. Mrs. Chanel had passed on, Thomas had told her, and he missed her dearly.

An hour after Doctor Trout arrived, Alyssa was sitting on the king-sized bed waiting for him to tell her his findings. He had poked and prodded her, tisking the entire time. She remembered him from when he would come to see her dad. He was old even then and was positively ancient now.

He still had those eyebrows that looked as if they had a life of their own. She remembered thinking as a child that if he could get them moving fast enough, he would be able to fly. While his brows still defied anything she'd ever seen, he was grayer than she remembered and much older-looking

"You're in very good shape for a dead woman. A little under nourished, and beat the hell up, but otherwise all right. Mind me asking where you been for the past nine years?"

"Yes, I do. What do you mean 'dead woman?'" Dr. Trout had been making notes on a pad of paper, as Thomas had asked him to not put this in any record until he let him know.

"Well, what was it, Thomas, about four years ago? Your mother claimed she had proof you were dead. Then about a year ago, she even had this 'doctor'"—Dr. Trout made the quotation signs with his fingers—"say he had discovered your dead body in an abandoned cave in the northern part of Ireland."

Alyssa fought the smile. "And where is my body now? I'm sure that it's still not in this cave, is it?"

"Funny thing that. You just up and disappeared when the coroner arrived. Now I know why." Dr. Trout sat in the big chair and looked at her. "The gash on your head looks to have been stitched by someone who knew what they were doing, same with the wound on your belly. The bruises around your neck are as recent as today and will only get worse over the next few days. I would really like to think that Nathan Howard's daughter is not doing anything stupid."

Alyssa glanced at Thomas, who stood and left the room. "Yes, I've been stupid. Stupid about a lot of things, but not anymore. There are some…I need to ask you something. It's personal."

"All right. If this has anything to do with your mother, then I agree. Whatever you want to do to her, I will back you one hundred percent. Nothing is too evil for her."

Alyssa burst out laughing. "No, not about my mother, but it's good to know I have your support where she is concerned. No, I need to know...I had...I had unprotected sex and I need to know how long before I can see if I'm pregnant."

~CHAPTER FOURTEEN~

Cain spent all day on Saturday setting up his office at the Grant Building. Damon told him that he would take care of putting an ad in the paper on Wednesday advertising that he had taken on a new partner and that Doctor Cain Waite, MD was looking for patients. That had been on Friday morning after Cain had taken his sisters home from the hospital.

"You can follow me around on my rounds and such. Get to know the staff and a few of my patients at the office and by the beginning of next week, you should have a few people of your own. I anticipate you having a great many younger women flocking...err, trying to see you once your picture comes out too."

Cain flushed with embarrassment. He had had this problem in Maine too for a short while. Once the women realized he wasn't going to ask them out, they began to stop asking him. He wasn't looking forward to it happening again.

"Maybe I should just wear a bag over my head until they get used to me."

"Nah. It's not just your pretty face, though Charlotte did comment on it quite a few times after dinner the other night. But it's the body. She said you have a...how did she put it?

Oh yeah, a 'great ass and tight pecs.' She told me I'd have to work out if I wanted to compete with you."

Cain looked over at Damon. The man was in great shape even if one didn't take in the fact that he was nearly sixty years old. Cain just shook his head. That was something he'd forgotten about the Grant men; they spoke their mind, no matter the subject.

Cain was still grinning about the conversation when his office phone rang. He almost didn't answer, but was worried about his sisters. He picked it up, barking his name as a greeting.

"Have you found her yet? Jazzie and I have been waiting for you to call and tell us all day."

Cain sat in his chair and rubbed his eyes. He was tired of going over this with them. He'd told them yesterday, several times as a matter of fact, that he wasn't going to look for Alyssa.

"No, Quinn, I have not. And I told you this morning before I left that I'm not going to either. She could have gotten you and Jazzie killed with her selfish behavior and I would rather not have someone in my life like that. End of discussion. Would you like me to pick up pizza on the way home?"

There was so much silence at the other end that Cain was sure she'd hung up on him. If he couldn't see that the time was still counting the length of the call, he would be positive of it. He started to say something when she finally spoke.

"I thought you'd say that. I had hoped that you wouldn't, but I thought you would. I'm not even going to ask you again to give her a chance to explain. Nor am I going to tell you that I think Mother and Father had something to do with us getting hurt again." This time, he could hear her crying. "I love you, Cain," and the phone went dead.

Cain sat there for several seconds before he got up and dialed home again. He was mad. He wasn't sure yet at whom, but he was. When no one answered the house phone, he tried Quinn's cell phone and it went directly to voice mail, so he tried Jazzie's. She answered on the first ring.

"Where's Quinn? I need to talk to her." He could hear Jazzie relay the message, but Quinn's reply was muffled and he didn't hear it.

"She said to tell you to fuck off. I'm not playing mediator now, Cain. You're both too old for me to tell you two what the other said. You two will work this out on your own. And for the record, I think she's right, you are an asshole." Then Jazzie hung up on him too.

He was still holding the phone in his hand when the other line rang in. He was pissed now and was going to give Quinn a piece of his mind. Pushing the button for the extension, he snarled in greeting.

"You hang up on me again and I swear to Christ that I will come there and beat your ass but good. I will not go and find her and I will not be manipulated into doing something just because you two get it into your head what I fucking should be doing in my own life. Understand me?"

"Yes, sir. But I just wanted to make an appointment to speak to you. I have something that belongs to you."

Cain closed his eyes against the twitching in his left eye. It did that when he was stressed and he hadn't been this stressed in some time. He looked at the caller ID now and thought that he should have done that before.

"I'm very sorry. Do you have any sisters, Mr...?"

"Miller, sir. Thomas Miller. No, no, I'm an only child. Why do you ask?"

"Would you like some? No, I'm sorry about how I answered. My sisters are...appointment, you needed an appointment. I'm not...let me find something to write on. I can set you up with me anytime this week. I'm not officially taking patients yet."

"Oh, no. No, I'm not a patient, Dr. Waite. I have something to give to you. I could come by sometime mid-week if that would be convenient for you?"

Cain sat down again. Give to him? He was sure he didn't know that name. Maybe he was someone from his past when he'd lived here as a teenager. He was about to ask when the man spoke again.

"Dr. Waite, you don't know me. We've never met. I'm just to bring you this and we shall part ways. Would Monday be convenient for you?"

"Sure. That will be...am I in some sort of trouble, Mr. Miller? Should I have a lawyer when you come in?"

There was that silence again. "If you'd like. There really isn't anything you're in trouble for, Dr. Waite. I assure you."

"All right then, Mr. Miller. I'll see you at ten on Monday then."

~~~

"Miss, I have an appointment with Dr. Waite on Monday morning. I have instructed the bank to honor the request when he is ready to use it." Thomas set the tray on the desk she had been sitting at since noon and looked up at him. "Are you sure this isn't something you should be doing?"

Alyssa was sure he was right, but she didn't think he'd see her. In fact, she was positive he wouldn't. Then she looked at the tray he'd set in front of her.

"Who do you think you're feeding? I swear, Thomas, if I have to stay here much longer, I'm going to weigh as much as this house in no time."

In addition to the two ice cold bottles of water, there was a green salad with tomatoes and cheese. There was a large basket of club crackers and a bowl of what looked like minestrone soup, steam billowing off the top. When she lifted the lid covering the plate, she found a large baked potato with butter and sour cream, two thick, grilled pork chops with glaze on them, green beans with onions, and grilled tomatoes. Under the other cover was a slice of cherry pie that had to have been three inches thick and a quarter of the pie. Putting the top back over the pie, she looked at him again. He was not as innocent as he was trying to look.

"Dr. Trout said that you need to eat more. I'm just making sure that you do. And cook said that if you didn't like this, he could cook you something else. I do believe he is enjoying this. It's not often that he gets to cook for someone other than me."

Alyssa had been at this house for three days now. She had spent the first day sleeping. Now after resting for nearly thirty hours, she was ready to face the music. The papers had not mentioned her and she half expected the newspaper crews to be camped out in front of Thomas' door, but it was eerily quiet. When she had asked him about it, he had shrugged it off and moved on to another topic. She decided to try again.

"Thomas, how are you keeping this quiet? I know by now several people have to know what happened, yet there has been nothing on the news or in the papers about the murder of that man and the injuries of Quinn and Jazzie. And I won't be put off again."

"You will need to make a donation to the paper when this is over and to the policeman's charity. Captain Grant has requested to speak to you before that happens, but I have been able to put her off. I have explained that you needed your rest from your ordeal and your injuries."

"And the reason for my 'ordeal,' is she aware of that also? Or is she only concerned because the Waite girls were hurt?"

Alyssa could tell by his face that he wasn't happy about her tone. She flushed. To be honest, neither was she. To make it up to him, she picked up her fork and knife and began cutting into the chop.

"The board meeting is set for Friday morning. I have made sure that your mother and uncle are not aware of it and won't be informed until they come in on Friday morning. The Sinclair Group will also be there, as well as three other of your holdings. I have been able to make contact with most of the other holdings and have set you up with appointments with them next week." Thomas pulled out a pad of paper. "You also have an appointment with a stylist for your hair tomorrow and Miss Ryland is coming in later this afternoon to fit you for a new wardrobe."

Alyssa finished chewing before she answered. The pork chop was delicious and she was nearly finished with the first one before she realized she'd eaten it. And most of the potato.

"They all know to keep quiet, right? I'm sure you explained, but I'm sort of nervous. I can't...Thomas, you'll be there, right?"

He put his pad away, sat up straighter in the chair, and regarded her. Alyssa was never one to squirm, but he was making her nervous and she hated that feeling. He stood when she put down her fork and knife.

"I cannot, miss, and you know it. I will be just outside the door if you should need me, but I—"

"I do need you, Thomas. Please come into the meeting with me? It's been so long that I'm not sure that...I don't want to make my father regret this, leaving this all to me."

Thomas sat back down again. Hard. Alyssa was sure she had heard his teeth clamp together when he had.

"Alyssa Howard, your father was very proud of you and there is nothing in this world that you could do that...he loved you. With all his heart he loved you. And anything that happens in that closed room will be fine. Your father knew what he was doing when he left you in charge of the company. You'll make him proud."

Alyssa could only nod as he stood, kissed her forehead, and gathered up the tray. She barely managed to hold onto her tears until he left the office. Thomas believed in her and what she was doing. He may not have wanted her to be gone so long, but he believed in her. She opened the next file in front of her and couldn't see anything through the tears. She would make her father proud of her if it was the last thing she did.

Groaning when she realized what file she had opened, she nearly closed it when something caught her eye. Her mother's expenses, usages of credit cards, and the bank statements were clipped to each side of the folder. Flipping through the rest of the bank statements, Alyssa started to grin. By the time she had gone through the entire year of them and the credit card expenditures, she was smiling. Her mother had been a very busy woman since Alyssa had been gone. Picking up the phone, she called Thomas back in.

"Where are my mother and Uncle Samuel staying right now? I can see that Nathan is in rehab and that Robert is in Europe," she asked him as he settled in a chair.

"Let's see, your mother is in the mansion and has been since the day after you disappeared. I believe your uncle Samuel has been as well. They have let go most of your staff and have replaced it...I think there has been a succession of help there since you've been gone. Why do you ask?"

Alyssa looked at Thomas. She knew then that he'd put this particular file on top because he knew something. What, she didn't know, but she was more than willing to figure it out. With his help, of course.

"According to my dad's will, they were to be 'put out,' I think were his exact words. Why are they allowed to continue to stay there? And why"—she picked up the file again and showed him the pages she had marked—"are there huge payments to me monthly from the household account? The one that I own, I would like to point out."

Thomas grinned. Then he chuckled. "You are your father's daughter. Yes, they are paying you rent. And yes, from your own accounts. I believe they were advised to do that from their attorney, Charles Winegardner. I was informed that he thinks it will establish them as to not 'sponging' off you, but actually renting from you."

Alyssa looked at the file again. Seriously? Her mother was paying her rent from Alyssa's account to live in a house that Alyssa owned.

"And the expenses? I suppose I'm being equally generous in paying those as well?" She knew the answer even before she asked. She had the accounts in front of her.

"I believe that is so as well, miss. You are a very sweet person, I've heard, and would like nothing but the best for your poor mother in her time of need. Your uncle as well."

Alyssa snorted. She couldn't help it. She was neither sweet nor wanted the best of anything for either of them.

"I need an attorney. I need one that I can get started on taking this...this mess on without them alerting either the media or my dear mother and uncle. Do you have anyone in mind?"

Thomas' grin, this one more like a shark that has found a tasty meal, said that he had just the perfect person in mind. She didn't even want to know, but told him to have him or her here tonight if at all possible.

"Him. And I will. Shall I tell him that he will be a permanent fixture in your arsenal in the future, miss?" Thomas asked as he stood.

"Tell him he will have top billing if things go the way I want." As Thomas made his way to the door, she stopped him. "Thomas, I know I haven't said this yet. But thank you. I don't...I don't know why you've done this for me, but I thank you."

"Oh, miss, I did this for you because I love you. You and your father have been my friends since the day he asked me to come and work for him. And you? Why, you are the spitting image of him in both mind and face—though you are much prettier. But you are very welcome. I shall have Andrew Miller meet you this evening."

Alyssa burst out laughing when the door closed behind him. She thought she might have just hired Thomas' son.

~CHAPTER FIFTEEN~

Cain was sitting in his office at nine-thirty on Monday morning when there was a knock on his door. He wanted to tell whoever it was to go away, but people, especially the nurses, had been coming by at least twice an hour since he'd started in the office that morning at five. His head hurt. The door opened without him saying anything. It was Damon.

"You look like shit. Have you found out where Quinn has gone yet?"

"No. And Jazzie still isn't speaking to me. She moved into the cottage and now I don't see her either. If I didn't see her car out in front every night when I come home, I wouldn't know she was still there. And then yesterday, Gracie Anne called me and ripped my head off."

Cain had five sisters. All younger than him and mean as rattlesnakes, he was beginning to realize. Each of them, with the exception of Sin, had called him once a day to berate him for not contacting Julie...Alyssa.

But Quinn leaving hurt him more than he wanted to admit. They were twins and closer than the others. He supposed that Lilly-pad and Sin were just as close, as they were identical twins, but he couldn't ask them either. When he spoke, or rather when they spoke, he couldn't get a word in edgewise.

"Nicky and I had a falling out. It was just after we found out that Morgan was pregnant with his twins. He and I didn't have a civil word passed between us for months. Even during the delivery I wasn't happy with him, either of them, as a matter of fact. You need to think about why she isn't speaking to you and fix it. Family, especially yours, needs each other." Damon stood to leave. "By the way, you have a patient in the lobby. Dapper little man with a briefcase. Something I should know?"

"No. I don't...he says he has something for me. He called on Saturday when I was in here setting up the office. His name is Thomas Miller. Do you know him?"

"Nope. I'll have Carol show him back if you're ready." At his nod, Damon left.

When the door opened again, Mr. Miller was standing there saying something to Carol. They knew each other, it appeared, and Cain made a mental note to speak to her about Mr. Miller after this was over.

"Dr. Waite, thank you for seeing me. I won't take up much of your time. There is just a matter of giving you this check and then I'll be on my way."

"Check? I don't...perhaps you should tell me why you're giving me a check before I accept it." Cain eyed the envelope that Mr. Miller had in his hand with suspicion. Cain was startled when the older man burst out laughing. He sat down in one of the chairs and put the envelope on his desk.

"She said you wouldn't just take it. She told me that I'd be lucky if I was able to get out with my hair in place. Are you a violent man, Dr. Waite? No, don't answer that, I can see that you are not. The check, or checks in this case, are the reward for finding Miss Howard—two million plus a bonus for her being alive."

Cain could only stare at him. Two million? A reward? Bonus? He sat back in his chair and regarded the man. "I don't want her money. If that's all you came here for then you—"

"No, it's not. Miss Howard told me that you wouldn't take it. The money is yours, Dr. Waite. I either give it to you, or your mother and father. And I know from my sources that you do not want that to happen. May I tell you something?"

"Yes, but it's not going to change my mind. I don't care who you give it to. Alyssa isn't buying her way back into my good graces with her money. She could have gotten my family killed with her stubbornness and as it is now, a man is dead."

"Yes. Mr. Pochak. Unfortunate, that. But he did harm my mistress. And your family as well. Were you aware that your parents hired him and that other man? Ah, I can see that you were not. Yes, Mr. Pochak and his partner were cell mates of your father's when he was in prison recently. He hired them to get Miss Howard at all costs." Cain watched as Mr. Miller opened his briefcase and pulled out a file. "Here is the transcript of the phone conversation after the failed attempt. It's is very…how should I say…graphic." Cain took the file. "I have made sure that the police have a copy, so you may have that one. As for the attempt, Miss Howard has been in hiding for almost a decade from her mother. I cannot divulge the circumstances surrounding the reasoning just yet, but it was either flee or become her uncle's wife." Mr. Miller stood. Cain did as well. "I will take my leave, Dr. Waite. If you have any questions, my number is on the folder, as is my address. I have a house guest right now, but I'm sure that we could meet without her knowledge. Good day."

Before he could get to the door, his office phone rang and without thinking, he picked it up. The caller ID said it was Quinn and he wanted, no, he need to speak to her.

"Quinn, where are you, baby? I'm so sorry, please tell me—"

"Well ain't that just sweet as curdled milk, my boy loving his little sister. You make me wanna puke."

"What the fuck do you want and why do you have Quinn's cell phone? If you have her so help me—"

"Shut the fuck up and listen. I ain't gonna tell you this more'n once. You will get that bitch to give you my money or I'll kill her. Ain't got no problem with that. You tell that bitch that I want my money or Quinn is dead. I ain't fucking around no more."

Cain was barely aware that Thomas sat back down in the chair again. He didn't say anything, but Cain looked up at him and he knew that Thomas had figured out that something was wrong. He couldn't think past his father's voice and what he was saying.

"You harm her and I'll kill you. I kid you not, I will."

"Listen to the big doctor, gonna take someone's life. You'll do well to listen to your daddy, boy. I don't want to hurt Quinn, but I will. I need that money. I'll call you back in one hour. You tell that bitch I want ten million or she has another death on her hands. It ain't gonna be my fault, but hers, you hear me?" Then the line went dead.

Cain looked over at Thomas; he had no choice. "My father just kidnapped my sister and is holding her until I get Alyssa to give him ten million dollars."

Thomas didn't bat an eye, but stood up, pulled out is cell phone, and left the room. Cain couldn't even focus on what he was saying his heart hurt so badly. His father, his own father, had just told him that he was going to kill his own flesh and blood for money. When Thomas came back into the room, Cain simply looked at him.

"Dr. Waite, do you hear me? Come now, all is not lost. Dr. Waite, you must pay attention. What is your father's plan?"

He looked at Thomas and wanted to cry. He knew that men didn't cry, but right now, he needed it more than anything. Then he thought of Alyssa. He wished...no, he couldn't begin to think she'd ever forgive him.

"He's going to kill his daughter if he doesn't get ten million dollars from me. I don't have it, Thomas. I used all I had to...that's all I have." Cain pointed to the envelope on the desk. "I'm sorry. You should go. I have to...I have things to do."

~~~

Alyssa hung up the phone and stared at the notes she had scribbled from Thomas. Quinn. Her own...Alyssa didn't want to think about what Cain must be going through and what he must be thinking. She stood and went to the bedroom.

Pulling on some socks and her dark tennis shoes, she thought about what she would need, where she would need to go. Discarding several shirts, she went to the kitchen to find the cook.

"I need some really worn clothes, Mike. And huge. Do you have anything here I can borrow? And I'll need a car, truck if there is one. Wait! I don't drive. I...fuck." He just grinned at her when she blushed. "Sorry," she said to him.

"Miss, I have someone who can drive you, as well as a truck. My son, he will be more than happy to take you where you need to go. As for the huge shirt, first I believe anything that I own would be huge on you. But I will have Billy bring you that as well. Anything else?"

Alyssa liked this man more and more. "No. Yes! I will need to go to a store. I don't have...you know who I am, don't you?" She had been living here for several days now and no one had used her name. She didn't know who Thomas trusted, but she was out of time. Cain needed her.

"Yes, miss. We all do. But you're safe here. What can I help you with?"

127

"I don't have any money."

Twenty minutes later, she was in Billy Oak's truck. She wondered if it would make it to the end of the drive much less to the store then back to the Howard Building. But Billy had told her that it was what was under the hood that counted and that he had a hemi or something there. She didn't say anything to that or when he stroked his truck. Wondering what other things she might have missed in ten years, she climbed into his truck armed with Mike's credit card and all the cash he had, nearly three hundred dollars.

"First thing we need to do is go to the store and purchase a few things. Then we need—" Her cell phone vibrated in her pocket making her squeal. It was Thomas.

"Miss, I've contacted Drew and he is going to meet you at the Howard Building. He will help you in any way that you need. Please be safe, miss. I do not wish to lose you again."

"I will. We're going to Wal-Mart now. Billy and I are going to get some things to help me find Quinn." She looked over at Billy then lowered her voice. "Is Cain all right? Does he...you didn't tell him, did you?"

"No, miss, I did not. Although I believe this to be a mistake, I will honor your wishes on this. If you need anything and neither man with you can help, call me and I will make it happen."

Alyssa was still grinning when she hung up. She'd heard Thomas say those words to her dad on many occasions. And Thomas usually did too.

The trip to Wal-Mart took nearly an hour. The clerks were very helpful, almost too helpful, in assisting them with loading the cases of water and fruit in the back of Billy's truck. She had heard from Thomas once during that time and again when they were stopping in the alley that ran along her building.

"Mr. Waite senior is demanding ten million in cash for the release of his daughter. He said that he will murder her and it will be your fault that he is not to blame. What would you like me to do here? Dr. Waite is not to contact the police, which he has said he won't."

Alyssa closed her eyes. She wanted more than ever to be with him, to hold him, but knew that he more than likely blamed her for this as well. She felt the tears well in her eyes again and turned away to see a man striding toward them in dark jeans and T-shirt.

"Hum, Thomas, if this man coming toward me is your son, he's younger than I thought."

Alyssa heard him chuckle. "That would be because Drew is my grandson. His father is a lawyer as well. Would you rather have the elder Andrew? I assure you, miss, Drew is hungry and ready to take on all that you need."

"No. Just surprised, that's all. I'm sure we'll work well...Thomas? I don't know how to thank you for all this. You've been so—"

"Come now, miss, we have a young lady to rescue. Let us keep focused, shall we? Drew has been made aware of what is happening. He is there to help you in any way you see fit. Now, let us get Miss Waite home, shall we?"

Alyssa wiped at the tears and closed the phone. She knew he was right. Getting Quinn back to her brother was paramount.

~*CHAPTER SIXTEEN*~

Cain stayed at the office, waiting. It had been two hours since his father had called the first time and forty minutes since the second call. Thomas stayed with him for the most part. They had kept Damon out of the loop, both knowing that he would alert Cait of what was going on. Every once in a while, Thomas would leave the room then return a few minutes later. Cain's father was supposed to call back and give him the location to drop off the money. Thomas said that he had called his bank and Cain had all that he needed to get his sister back.

His father. Cain had never hated his father as much as he did right now. He couldn't imagine hurting your own child, much less holding them for ransom. Cain wished that he could talk to Quinn. Then he thought of Alyssa and about how much he'd really like to speak to her.

He knew that he had treated her badly, had said things that he shouldn't have. He wished he could take them back, wished he could tell her how sorry he was. But she was out of his league. A wealthy woman like her didn't date country doctors like him. Especially ones with a family like his.

His family was everything to him. Not so much his parents, but his sisters were. The six of them had grown up hard and fast. He and Quinn were perhaps the closest. They being twins probably had something to do with that, but not entirely.

Quinn used to work for an office as a receptionist, but when he had left Maine, so had she. He knew that she was looking for a job and wished now that he had paid more attention to if she had found one. He knew that she had single-handedly run the place because the president of the company had begged Cain to stay so that Quinn would. He supposed it had something to do with her ex-husband Carl, but he didn't know for sure.

Grace Anne, or Gracie Anne, his younger sister by only sixteen months, worked in New York. She had worked for a large clothing manufacturer that sold knockoffs of designer clothing to women who couldn't afford the real thing. Then she started making and designing her own line. She was known all over the world as Gracie Anne to some of the richest women in the world. He didn't understand her job, he thought with a grin. To him, a dress was a dress and who cared who had worn it? But he did love the feel of his silk and linen suits, so who was he to complain?

Jazzie, or Jasmine Zinnia, was a...Cain had to chuckle when he thought of her. She had a sort of checkered work history and couldn't hold a job for long. She had at one time run a very successful restaurant kitchen for about six months. Cain didn't really care so long as she was happy because she hadn't been for so long.

Lilliane Iris, or "Lilly-pad" to her family, was an identical twin, but the polar opposite of her mate. Lilly-pad was fun and carefree where her sister, Sydney, "Sin," was not. Lilly-pad lit up a room when she entered, which was probably why she made a great teacher. Cain thought that Sin would just as soon light up one with a flame thrower. He loved them both and loved the differences his sisters had.

He was still thinking about them when his office phone rang again. He didn't recognize the number this time and was hesitant in answering it. Thomas was gone so he didn't have to worry about him, so he picked it up on the third ring. He was both surprised and terrified when he heard Spencer Grant's voice.

"Cait wanted me to call you and see if you've heard from your dad. She and her team are searching right now for Quinny and didn't want you to worry."

Not worry. He wasn't even sure if that was possible right now. But he knew that screaming at Spencer, Cait's husband, would do no good. Then he wondered who had told the police and he started to worry. "How did you know? He said not to call the police. Christ! He'll kill her, damn it. I want to know who called the police."

"Thomas Miller did, but no one knows but Cait. No one, Cain. He called us at home and let us know. He told us what was going on and that you needed us. I swear to you, we are doing nothing that would lead anyone to believe that the police are involved."

Thomas again. The man seemed to know just what to do. Cain leaned back in his chair again and closed his eyes. It was suddenly too much, too much of everything.

"I'm very worried. I haven't heard from my…how could he do this, Spence? How could a man…his own child? He said he would kill her if I didn't get him the money."

"I know, Cain. I'm so sorry. Some people just don't deserve what they have. You take my number and as soon as you hear anything, call. We're all here for you, buddy."

Cain hung up a few minutes later and stayed where he was. When the door opened again, he didn't even bother looking up. He knew Thomas' quiet way as well as he did his own right now.

"That was Spencer Grant. He told me that he and Cait were doing everything they could to get her back." He heard the chair sigh as it did when someone sat in its comfort. "I don't know how to thank you for all that you've done. I just…thank you very much. I hope your boss knows what a treasure you are."

Thomas chuckled. "I believe my boss knows just what I am. Miss Alyssa will be pleased to know that I've helped you in your time of need, Dr. Waite."

"It's Cain. Alyssa? Is she…is she all right?" He had wanted to ask all morning, but he just didn't know how to do it. Cain opened his eyes and looked at Thomas.

"She is rested. Her wounds are healing. She doesn't seem to be—"

The phone ringing cut him off and Cain felt his body tense up. Before he could answer, Thomas' cell phone rang as well. When he looked down at it, Thomas stepped out of the room again. Cain picked his phone up.

"You got me that money, boy?" his father asked as soon as Cain identified himself.

"Why are you doing this? Quinn is your own daughter. I'm your son, how can you do—"

"This isn't about you. Ain't about your sister either. It's business. I need that money as sure as I'm a' standing here. And I found her. She thinks she so high and mighty to hit a man in his own sons' house. Well I showed her, didn't I? You bring that money to this here house on Molly Rock Lane. You know where it's at. It's at the house right there on the corner. You hear me?"

"Yes, and I want to talk to Quinn. Now. You put her on the phone or I'm not budging." Cain knew he would do whatever it took, but he needed to talk to Quinn.

"You just do as you're told. You drop it right where I telled you and we'll see if you are listening to your daddy. If'n I see one car that I don't know, you're gonna force me to kill her. Hear me?"

"Yes, and you hear me you miserable excuse for a human being. If there is one bruise, one cut, even one small scrape on her body, I will hunt you down and rip you apart.

You hear me?" Cain slammed the phone down and looked up at Thomas who was standing in the door way.

"I guess you have a drop point, Dr. Waite?"

~~~

The group with Alyssa had been passing out water and fruit for an hour when she finally noticed Moon and Toby. She didn't know whether to give him a hug or shake him. Whenever the churches came by with fruit or blankets, Moon or Toby or even both would be the first in line. Today, they decided to wait. Damn it.

"Moon, you scared me. I was worried about you. How are you doing?"

He looked at her for several moments. She knew she looked different and waited until he either gave up and asked or figured it out on his own. Toby finally leaned over and whispered something to his partner that had Moon look at her sharply.

"Miss Rocky? That you? My oh my, you sure enough clean up good, don't you? You find yourself a good pimp?"

Alyssa put her hand on Drew's arm to hold him back. She was sure that Thomas had told him to stick to her like glue because he had done exactly that. The only time he had left her with more than three feet between them was when she went to the bathroom and then he'd been right outside the door.

"No. I've come into a little money. I have you some fruit, Moon. A whole bag of oranges for you and Toby, but I need something from you. Trade me?"

Moon did not like to take charity. He honestly didn't. He would go to the shelter every week for his meal, but he would stay and clean up afterward, sometimes mopping up the shelter floor after everyone had left. Moon was a good man.

"Trade, huh? What kind of trade? And I ain't going to go to no more meetings either if that's what you'ra thinking.

Me and Toby, we got more things to do than to sit and hear some jack wipe talking about the Bible like he done read it. I read it and I ain't never seen some of the things that man said was in there."

"I know. You showed me, remember? No, I'm looking for someone Crackers might have been with. A man who was hurt maybe."

Alyssa had known who the men were that tried to drag her from the car. Crackers, or Pochak, as the police had called him, and his partner Angel. Alyssa wasn't sure of Angel's real name, but he went by that because of the tattoo on his face and neck. It was of an angel. Crudely done, it covered about half his face. Alyssa and Rodney thought it had been done in prison, but neither had cared enough to ask.

"Nah. I ain't seen him since…when was it, Toby? 'Bout three days now, I'ma guessing. He had him some flash, but I don't know where he got it either."

Money. So Crackers had some money. Probably his payment for getting her, she thought. It would be like him to be that stupid as to go around showing people what he had. It was then that Alyssa noticed that Lily was staring at her from across the squatter's lot. She started toward her when Lily pointed to the building on her right and headed to her left. Grabbing up a bag of oranges, Alyssa made her way to the building.

Alyssa trusted Lily. She had never done anything to harm her and had stayed out of her business. That wasn't the norm with people like Lily. More often than not, they would get into your business so deep you'd have to ask them updates about your life. Smiling, Alyssa turned just in time to see Drew coming with her.

"No. You stay here. I need you to hand out the water and fruit for me. We need to establish some good will with these people."

Drew just put his arms over his chest and cocked a brow at her. Alyssa wondered if that pose was something that men just knew or if it was something they got passed down from their fathers. It was something she promised herself she would never allow her own sons to do.

"I don't think so. I was told to stay with you as if we were joined at the hip. You walking away from me, that doesn't give me all that much of a warm and fuzzy feeling. Besides, those are my granddad's orders."

"And you always listen to your granddad I suppose. I can't have you with me. I have to...I'm meeting someone and you have to stay..." Alyssa looked up in time to see Cait Grant and a man coming toward her. "Christ, who all did you invite to come down here?"

Alyssa stood, waiting for them to get to her. She wasn't happy either, it appeared. That thought made Alyssa feel just a little better, but not entirely.

"Hello, Miss Howard. Beautiful day for a kidnapping, wouldn't you say? Anything we can help with? Oh, this is my husband, Spencer. Spencer, this is Alyssa Howard, the woman I was telling you about."

Alyssa wasn't even going to ask about *his* brow thing. She was going to ask Thomas about it next time she saw him. Then it occurred to her what she'd said.

"Help? What do you...Thomas. I'm going to fire him. He needs to...I have to go and meet someone. And this"— she pointed to Drew—"won't let me."

"Doctor and Captain Grant, how are you this afternoon? Granddad said I was to stay with her no matter what. I think he thinks she'll get into trouble. I think he might be right."

Alyssa wanted to kick something. Preferably Drew's kneecaps. "Hello? Standing right here. Damn it, I have to go. If you follow me then I might miss a lead. Stay here or she might...she doesn't like men, all right?"

"I'll go. I can stay with her and try to keep her out of trouble too. Come on, Miss Howard, lead the way."

"Stop calling me Miss Howard. In fact, don't call me anything. You might find that...no one knew my name here. Well, except for Rodney. They don't want...we are very private people here." Alyssa looked over to where she was supposed to meet Lily and sighed. "Damn it, all right, but you have to be quiet and stay out of my way. I mean it. Lily isn't going to be happy about this any more than I am."

With a quick "careful" from Spencer, Alyssa and Cait were on their way to the building. Alyssa tried again to get Cait to let her go alone and she simply shrugged. Alyssa decided that she needed to get herself a gun. Maybe if she carried one, she'd be safer to these people. Probably not, she thought with a wry grin. She'd probably shoot one of them first.

Lily was in the basement of the building having come in from the back end to meet with Alyssa. She didn't say anything to Cait, but she did nod to her. When Alyssa and Lily walked a few feet away, Cait stayed back. Lily took the bag of oranges and hugged them to her body as though they were precious gold.

"Thank you. I knew you were not from here. You always had a...an air about you. Not that you was a snob, just you seemed too good for the streets." Lily looked over at Cait. "She's a nice police person. I ain't never had no beef with her."

Alyssa looked over at Cait. "I suppose. I don't really know her. She's a pain in my ass right now, though." Alyssa looked back at Lily, who was holding the oranges to her nose again. "You need anything? I'm going to have blankets brought down soon. I'll make sure you get one."

"I want a job. You think...I want to work somewheres and get myself fixed up. You think...can you help me with that?"

A job? That was the last thing that Alyssa thought she'd ask for and decided that she would find her one, even if she had to create one for her. Yes, a job would be something...Later, she told herself. She would think about that later.

"You come to the Howard Building on Monday morning. Can you be there at eight o'clock? Good. I'll have them ready for you. I have something to do this week yet and I have to find a friend of mine."

Lily nodded. "You looking for that pretty girl you was shopping with? I know where they have her."

~*CHAPTER SEVENTEEN*~

"Dr. Waite?" Cain sat up, startled away by the voice in the dark. It took him several seconds to remember where he was.

"Yes. Thomas, I'm sorry, I must have dozed off. I...what is it?"

"Your sister is on her way to the hospital. She is fine, just a few cuts and bruises. But I'm afraid there's some...well, sir, there is some bad news. I'm afraid there has been a shooting. Captain Grant will speak to you about it, but your father...I'm afraid he's been shot. He has been rushed to the hospital as well."

Cain sat up. All he could think of was that Quinn was all right and he wanted to talk to Alyssa. He wished that he could see her and have her with him.

"I have to get to her. I...what happened? How did they find her?" Cain asked as he stood and stretched.

"I'm afraid I'm not at liberty to say. Captain Grant has requested that I bring you to the hospital. She is of the opinion that you will be much safer as a passenger than as a driver. We can leave when you are ready."

They left for the hospital soon after. It was bright out, almost like mid-day. He hadn't realized that it had gotten so late. Looking at his watch, he realized that it was well past three o'clock. He must have been asleep for a couple hours.

He couldn't believe it, but he hadn't been sleeping so well of late so that could explain it.

Cain had been thinking about Alyssa and his treatment of her. He had not been a nice guy and he hadn't given her a chance at all. Glancing over at Thomas, he wondered what the man would say if he asked if his "house guest" was Alyssa. He knew it was. Deep in his heart, he knew this man knew where she was. Then there was the money.

The envelope that Thomas had given Cain had had ten checks in it. All made out to Cain and all for the same amount, two hundred thousand each. It was the two million dollar reward for the information on Alyssa Howard, the missing heiress Thomas had told him. However, it was the bonus that amazed him. This check was for another two million alone. The bonus, Thomas explained, was because Miss Howard had been found alive.

"I hadn't realized she was missing, or an heiress, much less one that could have been dead. Why the bonus?"

Thomas had looked uncomfortable and Cain hadn't thought he would answer. "I'm not at all sure that my mistress would appreciate me telling you this story, sir. You should speak to her. It is a dreadful tale, I'm afraid, and I don't know all the details. Suffice it to say that she was correct in disappearing for a time."

So Cain had four million dollars in an envelope in his jacket pocket and was on his way to the hospital to make sure his sister was all right.

Quinn was in a private room being examined by Damon. He hadn't been aware the man knew about what had been going on, but seeing Cait there made him realize that there was more going on than he'd known. He glanced over at Thomas on his way to see his sister and noticed that the man had a look of concern on his face. He didn't have time to think about that much as he saw Quinn in the next moment and took her into his arms.

"Cain! Oh, Cain, hold me, please? I was...he hit me. Father...he was...oh, Cain, just hold me, please?"

Jazzie was there and a woman that he didn't know, but his sisters did. He simply held Quinn as she cried. Jazzie crawled up into the bed with Quinn and he held them both. Everyone but the woman slipped out of the room.

Quinn lifted his sister's chin and looked at her face. It was bruised and her lip had been split at the corner. There was a mark on her chin, like the beginnings of a bruise, but she looked good to him. He held her tighter to him and closed his eyes. She was back.

"Cain, I can't breathe. I love you too, but I need to breathe and I'm all right. I promise, I'm all right."

"Tough. I'm holding you and you'll just have to live...are you really all right, Quinn? Really? I was...Christ! He took you. He actually took you. How...no, I don't care how he got you. I'm just glad you're here now."

"He had her tied up in the basement. I saw him and Angel take her. They had her tied to a beam. I couldn't get her by myself but then Sa...then the police came in and saved her," the woman in the corner said quietly.

Cain felt his sister stiffen in his arms and drew back to look down at her. "What? What happened that you're planning to tell me? I know that look, Quinn Susan Waite. You can't hide something from me."

"I'm fine, that's all that matters, right? The...Damon said I can go home tomorrow. He wants to make sure that I'm—"

"Quinn? Tell me, please? Does this have anything to do with Father being shot? I didn't get any details, but I know that he's the one who took you." Cain looked at the woman. "Who were you going to say? You said 'Sa,' who could...Sally. You mean Alyssa Howard, don't you? Christ! Was she hurt? Quinn, was Alyssa hurt too?"

"No. Not hurt too badly. She...she's going to be angry with us. Alyssa shielded me from...when Cait shot those men, she, Alyssa, shielded me with her body. Angel hit her, but it wasn't...she saved me. Lily told her where I was and she saved me."

Quinn was sobbing now and Jazzie was too. Lily stood and Cain thought she was coming to the bed when she slipped out the door. He pulled from his sisters and went after her.

"Miss? Wait, please? You helped save my sister. I don't...you have to let me repay your kindness. I don't know...she's my sister." Cain felt the words were inadequate for what he felt, but the woman seemed to understand him. She moved back to him and seemed unsure of how to hug him, because he could see that was what she wanted...no, he realized, she needed to do. He pulled her into his arms and hugged her to him. After several seconds, she hugged him back, ferociously.

"She told us to not say anything. She said you'd be mad that...Sally ain't going to give me a job now, I just know it. Sally...Alyssa she said her real name is—she said she'd help me find a job, but she is hurt too and nobody cares what she did. They care." Lily pointed back to Quinn's room. "Angel hit her in the back real hard when he seen that the police where there. He yelled that it wasn't fair."

Cain watched as Cait Grant walked toward them, Spencer close behind. Lily pulled away when she saw them coming as well.

"Cain. Lily, Miss Howard is going to be upset with you for telling on her. But I'm certainly glad you did. If she won't give you a job, Spencer and I will. But I don't think that'll be an issue if Cain here does it right. Will it, Cain?" Cait winked at him and he grinned.

"I'm certainly going to do my best. I think I know where to find her too. If you ladies will excuse me and Spencer…shit, my sisters. I have to…"

"You go on, Cain. I'll take care of them. I'm sure they will be thrilled you're going to fix this too. Alyssa is hurt, by the way. I tried to get her to come here so that Damon could look at it, but she just climbed into the monster truck of Drew's and took off. If it's any consolation, I don't think he's very happy with her either," Spencer told him with a grin.

"Drew? I don't think I know who that is."

"Thomas Miller's grandson, Andrew Miller. I think she had just hired him this morning as her lawyer. Not so sure if he still is. She was cussing him out the whole time he stuffed her into the truck. That boy was pissed. He told her that he'd been sent to protect her and his granddad was going to strip his hide off him."

Everything suddenly fell into place. Thomas had been leaving the room to update Alyssa and get information from her. The money, there wasn't a bank, but Alyssa. She was going to provide the…

"Where's Thomas now? I'm betting he's with her. Spencer, I thank you for telling the girls. If you all will excuse me, I have a woman to win over."

Cain left the hospital. He wasn't sure where Thomas lived, but a short stop by the office and he not only had his address, but a phone number as well. He debated whether or not to call first then in the end, thought he'd better. If she was hurt, Thomas may have taken her somewhere else to be treated. Cain was going to have a bit of a talk with his little heiress.

"Yes, Dr. Waite, she's here."

Cain grinned at the tone. He would guess from it that Alyssa was pissing him off as well. "I'm on my way. It's probably best if you don't mention that. She is going to be pissed enough as it is."

The silence was almost funny. "I don't believe that would be possible at the moment, sir. She has a stubborn streak in her that I've...she is her father's daughter, I will say that for her. I do hope you will be able to make some headway into seeing to her for us. The household is in an uproar and Drew isn't helping."

Cain would bet he wasn't. He hadn't met the young man, but he already liked him. This was proving to be more fun than he'd hoped for.

"I'm on my way. I should be there in about ten minutes. I have my bag with me." Cain sobered quickly when he remembered what Lily had said. "Is she...are her injuries bad, Thomas?"

"No, sir, they are not. I do believe that she is hurting badly, but as for them being life-threatening, they do not seem to be. I cannot say for sure there won't be others before you arrive, but for now, she is up and about. I will hold my grandson back from further hurt until you get here. I've never...I had no idea two people could be so loud, sir."

Cain burst out laughing. He couldn't wait to get there. Hanging up his phone, he felt the smile slide momentarily off his face. His father had caused this and Cain had just realized that he'd not checked on him or his surgery. Cain wasn't even sure that he wanted to know right now, but picked up his phone again and called.

"I'm sorry, Dr. Cain, we've been trying to reach you. Your father didn't make it through the surgery. His wounds were great and he'd lost a great deal of blood as well. I did the best that I could under the circumstances."

"I understand. Is my mother there? Has she been notified?"

"Yes, Mrs. Waite is here. She has been sedated. She is taking if very hard. Are you coming in?"

The hopeful tone in the surgeon's voice, a Dr. Messer, would have been comical if Cain didn't know just how he felt. Cain's mother could take any situation and make it difficult, but losing her husband would be a blow to her. Roscoe was his mother's life. Well, above any feelings she had for her children, Roscoe came first and foremost in her life.

"I'm on my way to check on another patient that was injured when my father was. My mother is fine sedated. I will be in later to see her. Thank you, Dr. Messer. I know you did all you could."

After a few minutes more, they ended the call. Cain was just pulling onto Thomas' street when his phone rang again. It looked to be a hospital number. Thinking it was one of his sisters, he answered.

"Captain Grant just came in to tell me that Father is dead," Jazzie told him. "I'm not sure how I feel about that. He hurt Quinn, and Alyssa when he took Quinn. I feel bad for Mother, but him...I don't think I care. Does that make me a horrible person?"

"No. God, no. He never did anything for us to make us care one way or another, baby. And as for him being dead, I can't think past the part where he kept telling me that he planned to kill Quinn for money. No, honey, you don't need to feel remorse for not caring if he's dead or not."

"Cain...I was wondering about what Spencer said. He said that you were going to see about a woman. Is it Alyssa? If it is, do you think you can tell her thanks for me? She saved my life and she made sure that...I didn't see anything. Alyssa made sure that when Father came into the room and drew his gun, I never saw anything."

Cain had a great deal to thank Alyssa for. Shielding his sister from watching the police take out her father was just one of many things. In the two weeks that he'd known Alyssa, she'd done more for his sisters in terms of love and understanding than their mother had done in all their lives. Cain hoped to Christ Alyssa took him back. He didn't know what he was going to do without her.

"I'll tell her, Jazzie. I don't know if she'll speak to me, but I will let her know how much you appreciate what she's done. You rest now, and in the morning I'll take you back home. And Quinn, don't even think about living in that cottage. I want you at the main house."

With a small laugh, she assured him that she'd move back in with him, but that she was not sleeping in the brown room across from Jazzie. "I swear, Cain, it looks like someone fell into fresh mud, wore it in the room, and smeared it on everything in there. Looks just like brown poop if you ask me."

"All right, you don't have to sleep in there. I'll have it remodeled if it's that bad. Pick another room and we'll work from there."

"No, keep it. Sin will love it. It's all dark and dreary and weird like that fog movie is."

They laughed at that. Sin was in special services, and while they all loved her, she could be a little on the intense side.

"We'll see. I have to go and hope Alyssa won't hurt me while she cusses me out. I love you, Jazzie. So very much."

"I love you too, Cain. And don't fuck this up."

Sage advice, he thought. Very sage. He really hoped he didn't fuck this up with Alyssa.

~CHAPTER EIGHTEEN~

"I'm not ten years old and I would very much like it if you stopped treating me like I am. I'm a grown woman. And I—"

"Then how about you start acting like one? I swear to Christ you are the most...do you have any idea how terrified I was when I hear those gun shots? Christ, woman. Six fucking shots and—"

"Andrew Wayne Miller, you will watch your language in my home. And you..." Thomas pointed at her. "You will sit down before you fall down. I have never been so...if you plan to conduct meetings like this in the office, I shudder to think what the staffing will wonder. Andrew, I said to sit!"

Alyssa could tell Thomas was mad. But damn, it so was she. She was going to sit, but not if he told her to, especially if he told her to in that tone. Damn it, her back hurt.

In the past two weeks, she'd been beaten, cut, slapped around, and had had sex on a tile floor. The latter hadn't been all that much of a hardship, but still, it was on her list and she was not taking it off. Gingerly, she sat in the chair only to hop up again when the front doorbell chimed. Not another relative of Thomas. She didn't think she could take another person...It was Cain Waite.

"What's he doing here? Thomas? I swear if you called him here for whatever reason you can just...you can just un-call him."

Cain looked just too good standing there. His hair was tousled just right and the suit he had on reminded her of gray clouds on rainy days, the kind where you just wanted to stay in your jammies and snuggle up with a good book or a weepy movie, or both.

"Un-call? I don't even think that's a word. And as for what I'm doing here, I'm your physician. And as such, I can tell you right now there isn't a damned thing wrong with your lungs. I could hear you in the driveway."

Alyssa flushed. Okay, she'd been loud, but he still didn't have any reason to be here. Before she could tell him so, Thomas spoke.

"It is still my home, miss, and I will have who I want when I want. And right now, I want him to be here. He will examine you and you will co—if you say a single word, just one, miss, I will quit so quickly that you will not know what hit you. Sit." Alyssa sat.

When Thomas used that tone, it was as if her father had been standing there. She started to stand again, but he simply looked sharply at her. When Drew laughed, she was ready to blast him when Thomas started in on him.

"And you, young man, I did not pay for your fine education for you to talk like a guttersnipe. I would appreciate it if you would refrain from that sort of language in my presence. Also, I would have a word with you while the doctor examines Miss Alyssa."

"Grandda, you really can't expect me to be happy about what happened today. She could have been killed. I could have been killed. She is headstrong and needs her ass...her bottom blistered."

"You just try it, buck-o. In fact, you're fired. And Cain...Dr. Waite...he's not examining me. I've told you several times that—"

"Enough. I have spoken and you will obey. I have...you are more your father's daughter than even he thought, I believe. He would argue just to pass the time and I believe you would have given him a good run for his money."

"Thank you."

"It was not meant as a compliment and you very well know it. Now, I have a migraine and I wish for you to be silent for...for a day. He will examine you and you will cooperate. I'll not have any more nonsense this evening. Have I made myself perfectly clear, young lady?"

"Yes," she hissed at him. "But you will understand that I'm not happy about this or him. I thought you said someone was coming that would help me."

"And I have provided you with help. Now, Andrew, let us leave these two to this. I have a need for a brandy."

Alyssa glared at the two men as they walked out of the room. When the door shut with a quiet click, she turned to Cain. He was smiling. It was all she could do not to walk over and punch him right in the nose.

"I didn't ask him to bring you here and if you want to leave, he'd be all right with it. There isn't any reason for you to be here anyway. I'm fine."

"I don't mind being here. And we both know you are not fine. I want to examine you. We can start with your back. Quinn said you took a blow from my father there. May I see it?"

Alyssa stood up. She was fine sitting or standing. It was getting there that caused her pain. She tried to stop the look of pain she was sure he was seeing, but there was no help for it. She stood next to the chair and waited for him.

"I'll need you to take off your shirt. I can't see your back properly with it in the way."

There in lay the problem. She couldn't take the shirt off. Not without considerable pain, that was. She had tried to take the shirt off in the bathroom earlier, but she couldn't raise her arms up over her head enough to manage it. And she knew admitting it would be another failure in Cain's eyes, she was sure. Turning around to face Cain, she looked down at the floor. There was no way she wanted to see his aggravation at her again.

"I can't. I...the soreness is just across my shoulder blades and I can't lift up my arms enough to pull it over my head. Can't you just...I don't know, just lift it from the bottom and have a look? It's really not all that bad. I don't know why Thomas is making such a fuss about it."

Alyssa was startled when he lifted her chin up. More so when she saw what she thought was desire in his eyes. But she knew that couldn't be right, unless he just wanted to have sex with her again. That thought made her shift on her feet and a feeling of need moved over her body. Pulling her chin away from his fingers, she started to step away.

"Alyssa, I want you to look at me. Please?" It was the please, she decided, that had her turning back to him. It had sounded so sad, so hurt, that she looked back at him in spite of her need to get away.

She looked up at him. She would forever be fascinated with his eyes. They were beautiful and rich in color. Alyssa knew that she would never be able to look at jade again without thinking of him. And those curls. She actually had to clasp her fist shut so that she wouldn't reach up and brush them from his eyes. Reaching inside of herself, she tried to find something, anything that would distract her from him, at least long enough that she could get through this examination.

"Cut it from my back. I have some scissors here somewhere. Just cut if off and let's get this over with. I have things to do."

Cain stepped toward her and she thought he was going to get something to cut the shirt off her as she had asked. But he only moved closer to her. When she managed to step back about half a step before running into the chair behind her, he closed the distance between them.

"Thomas is correct, you know. You are very argumentative. Alyssa, may I kiss you? I've missed your taste and am only just now realizing how much I need more of you."

Alyssa felt her heart jump in her chest. Then she thought he was trying to hurt her, get back at her for hurting his family. She opened her mouth to tell him what he could do with his sense of humor when he closed his mouth over hers.

~~~

Cain felt her stiffen beneath him. Her mouth was firm and hard and he wondered if he was making a mistake in leaving himself and his body parts so exposed. But her hands on his forearms were soft and gentle. Moving closer to her and wrapping his hands around her, he pulled Alyssa close to his body, careful of her back.

He had only meant to brush his mouth over hers, a simple taste, a small kiss. But the moment he touched her, felt her breath over his skin, he was lost.

"Alyssa, please? Let me in, let me taste of you."

This time, when he touched his lips to hers, she ran her tongue along his lips, leaving them moist. Licking the taste of her from his mouth, Cain groaned deep within his chest, ran his hand through her hair, and pulled her to him. She was heaven, soft and warm, delicious and spicy. Their tongues dueled with each other, sliding along and through their mouths as they clung to each other. When Alyssa's hands curled in his hair, Cain lifted her up and her legs wrapped around him just as she jerked away from him. Pulling hard on his hair, she cried out.

"Alyssa, honey, I'm so sorry. I shouldn't have...let me go and I'll put you down. You can do it, honey. Loosen your grip on my hair and I'll be able to move again."

"I can't. Just let me...I need a minute. I'm sorry I'm hurting you, but the pain is horrendous."

Slowly, by degrees, she moved her fingers from his scalp. She wasn't really hurting him. It was the sudden change in what they had been doing from sensual heat to excruciating pain in a second.

Once she was standing next to him, Cain still holding her, he waited until her breathing was normal before he stepped back. He needed to look at her back now more than ever. "If your offer still stands, I'd like to cut away your shirt now. I think I need to take a good look at it and make sure there isn't anything more to what I've been told."

"It's really just a bruise, I'm sure. He hit me...I don't know what he hit me with, but it barely hurt at the time. It's only now that I can feel it. I'm sure it's nothing."

Cain could hear the pain in her voice and something else. Something he wasn't sure of. If he had to guess, he would say she was embarrassed. Of what he couldn't imagine, but that was what he heard. Getting his scissors out of his bag, he stepped up behind her and started to cut through the thin material.

As soon as her shoulder blade was exposed, Cain could see that it was much more than he'd first thought. The ugly bruise went across her scapula and over her spine. The more he cut away of the shirt, the more he couldn't believe she was standing up, much less walking around. The mark was about eight inches wide and went the entire width of her back from her right shoulder to just below her ribs on her left. The skin was not cut, but it was blue and red. He knew that she was in a great deal more pain than she was letting on.

"Alyssa, I want to take you somewhere where you can lie down. This is really bad, sweetheart, and I want to test to see if any ribs are broken. I don't think there are, but I want to make sure. I understand from Thomas that you can't go to the hospital, but I can take you to the office. I have everything I need there to make you more comfortable."

He wanted more than anything to scream and yell at someone. He wanted to go and find the man responsible for her injuries and beat the living shit out of him. More than anything, Cain wanted to hold her in his arms until it was all better.

"I can't. I don't think I can ride in a car again. Can't you just give me something for the pain? I'll be all right in the morning. You can leave, you know? Just tell me what to do and I'll fix it myself."

Cain couldn't help it, he burst out laughing. "No, baby, I can't. You are hurting and we both know it. Come on, let me get you to your bed. I can give you something there."

She led him to the staircase and waited for her to move up it. When she turned and looked at him again, he was sure he wasn't going to like what she was about to say. There was something there that made him think she was going to send him home. At least she was going to try to.

"There is absolutely no reason for you to hang around. Just give me a pain pill, or better yet, I'll get one from the bathroom. Thomas seems to have every over the counter drug in the world. I'll have him give you a call if I have any more problems. I want to thank you for—Cain! Put me down, you moron."

Thomas and Drew came around the corner just as she squealed. If she didn't stop squirming, he was going to drop her and then she really would hurt. As it was, not touching her back was making it extremely difficult to hold on to her.

"Hello, Thomas. I was wondering if you'd be so kind to point out which room is Alyssa's? She seems to have it in her head that I'm leaving and I'm not."

When she stopped struggling and stilled, he looked down. Her shirt was nearly off her and he could see her skimpy bra. With both her hands over her breasts, she couldn't move without falling. He turned her slightly so that neither Thomas nor Drew could see what she was doing.

"Oh, of course. She will need someone to keep an eye on her, I suppose. It's the last room on the left. There is a sturdy lock on the door as well. I believe I'd lock it behind you if I were you. Never know when she might…sleepwalk away from you again."

"Thomas Andrew Miller, you're fired. I never…what do you think you're doing telling him to lock me in? I'll…damn it, put me down. Andrew? I want you to sue him. I want him brought up on harassment charges right now. The idiot can't just cart me around like I'm a sack of potatoes. Andrew!"

They were at the top of the stairs when Andrew answered. "Sorry love, I don't work for you yet. In fact, you fired me an hour ago, remember? Sorry, just can't help you. Have a good night, Cain, and good luck. I think you're going to need it."

~CHAPTER NINETEEN~

It took her all of twenty minutes to calm down. The only good thing about it was that the pain receded when she was pissed off at Cain. So now that she was calming down, she was hurting again.

"I'm going to run you a bath then I'm going to have you soak in it for—"

"You so are not going to help me take a bath. I draw the line at having you wash me." She wanted to cry but wouldn't do it with him there. "Please, just go home. Your sisters probably need you. I know Quinn does. She asked for you several times when they were loading her in the ambulance."

"I'm not leaving, Alyssa. Besides, who do you think sent me here? Now hush up and let me help you. The bath will feel good then I'll give you something that will knock you out and you…"

"No! I can't…you can't drug me. I won't be drugged again. Never, you understand? Never again." She flushed. Cain stared at her for long moments before he nodded once and moved into the bathroom again. The water had been running since they had come up and she thought it was probably overflowing by now.

When he came back out with her robe in his hands, she knew that he was staying. She thought about stomping her foot, but didn't want to appear too childish. But she did growl at him when he dropped to his knees before her.

"I'm going to take off your pants, not attack you." He had them just to her knees when he finally asked what she thought he would when he'd first gotten there. "Are you really Alyssa Howard, the one who went missing all that time ago?"

"Yes. My father left me everything when he died. I was...my mother tried to have me have sex with my uncle and I left. Ouch." He'd pulled hard on her pants and jerked her around.

"I'm sorry. Seriously? Why?"

It was a rather personal question, but she answered him anyway. "My mother had several affairs when she was married to my dad. I didn't know he knew, not until they read the will anyway. My brothers, Nathan and Robert, aren't Daddy's either, just me. When Daddy died, he made sure that Mother knew about it. He cut them off, all of them. My uncle Samuel is my bro...is Nathan's father."

"So your dad got his revenge by leaving you everything. And the sex? Is she perverted or something?"

He got her panties off her and stood. For reasons she couldn't understand, she didn't feel timorous in front of him. Could be that they'd had sex, but she didn't think that was all of it.

"Probably. But that's not the reason. One of the stipulations in the will for my uncle to inherit was that he had to find a suitable wife and have a child. My mother told me that if he had a child with me, then when I was gone, she and my uncle would raise the baby."

They were in the bathroom now and Cain was helping her lower herself into the water when he stopped suddenly. She knew what had stopped him. It was the same thing that had made her run. The reason why she had stayed hidden for so long.

"What was going to happen to you that they'd need to raise the baby? Christ, and I thought my mother was bad. So you were going to sleep with your uncle, have his kid, and then what? Disappear? Fall ill and die? Your mother is a peach, Alyssa. A real peach."

She burst out laughing. His grin told her that that was what he'd planned. Once she was sitting in the water, she closed her eyes. It did feel good, actually, and she could feel her muscles beginning to tingle with warmth.

"She drugged me. That night, she drugged me. I was mad at her for making so light of Daddy's death that I didn't...no, that's not right. I never dreamed she'd do anything like she did. The tea was laced with something. As I tried to get away from the table, she told me that Uncle Samuel would have me, willing or not. I staggered toward the ladies room and threw up all over our waitress. Then I escaped out through the kitchen."

"And that's where you met Rodney Kincaid. He saved you, didn't he? He told you how to hide out and keep safe."

"Yes. I just found out from Thomas recently that he was aware of where I was the entire time. That he and Rodney took my pictures with different newspapers every so often to keep Mother from having me declared dead." Alyssa felt the tears as they fell. She didn't look at Cain, but kept her eyes closed. It hurt still, after all this time, what her mother had tried to do to her. More so that she'd been doing it with Alyssa's blessings. Her blessings because she couldn't bring herself to come home and confront her.

"What are you going to do now? I know that you are planning something. A woman like you doesn't come back without a ripple of news in the paper. She has to have something up her sleeve."

"I have a plan." She didn't want to tell him. She felt stupid enough at what she'd done in the first place that had caused the issues. She knew that whatever happened on

Friday was going to have repercussions for months, if not years.

Cain settled behind her on the floor. She didn't know what he was going to do until he asked her to sit up a bit. When she did, he poured water over her head with a plastic cup she'd brought in the bath a few days ago. When he started to wash her hair, soothing her in ways she'd never had before, he started talking.

"My father is dead. No, don't get up. He deserved whatever happened there. I don't know...I talked a bit with Quinn. She said that you saved her and that you shielded her from the actual shooting. I wanted to thank you for that."

As he rinsed her hair, she realized that he hadn't sounded like he was mad at her. Nor, now that she thought about it, did he seem like he blamed her. She turned to look at him when he sat back on the toilet.

"You don't blame me for his death? Why not?" Alyssa flushed. And before she could dive under the water and drown herself, he spoke again.

"No. I know that I did before. Blame you, I mean, but I don't. If I had listened to Quinn in the first place, none of this would have happened. Quinn tried to tell me that my parents were involved in the attack of you three the other day and I just wouldn't listen. I was blaming you for something that you'd had no control over."

Alyssa turned around in the tub before she started talking. "I'm...I was going to say that I'm sorry about your father, but I really am not. I'm sorry for your loss, but not that he's dead. Lily, another homeless person, told me where to find Quinn. She said that she'd seen Quinn and Crackers together in one of the abandoned warehouses on Lively Avenue a few hours before. I was going to go alone, but Drew and Cait wouldn't let me. I guess they were right. Quinn was tied up to one of the beams in the sublevels and

Angel was taunting her. I didn't know your father was there."

"Cait said that he had only just arrived when you and this Angel person had started to fight. She said that my dad was coming up behind you with a ball bat and was ready to swing it when Cait shot him the first time. I didn't know you knew them."

Alyssa turned slightly and looked at him. She decided that if he didn't want anything to do with her, she'd at least make sure he knew what had happened.

"Crackers, or Pochak, was a man who was more insane than most of us on the street. He'd been in and out of jail for a long time, longer than I'd been on the streets. Rodney said he'd been a punk all his life. He'd been a part of the murder that had killed his parents when he'd been a little boy."

"That would do it. Cait said that Angel's real name was Gus Deville and that he and Pochak had been cell mates to my father. They were supposed to split the money they got from you then part ways. Quinn running over Crackers put an end to the only one of them who had any sort of brains, if you can believe it."

Yes, she could believe that. Crackers was nuts, but Angel was nearly catatonic when Crackers wasn't around to get him moving. Once he did, there was no stopping him. Alyssa didn't know about Cain's father, but it made sense. They all seemed to be cut from the same cloth.

"I want to get out now. I don't suppose you'll leave, will you?" A part of her wanted him to go while a large part of her wanted him to stay.

"I'm not leaving you, Alyssa. We have a lot to talk about and I want to be with you. Let me help you out. Be careful now."

Cain helped her step out of the tub and wrapped her in a towel. Then he took another one and started to dry her hair. Alyssa felt tears pooling in her eyes again. No one had pampered her like this since she'd gotten sick as a child and her daddy had taken care of her. They went into the bedroom and she lay down on the bed, suddenly more tired than she'd ever been. She was asleep in a few minutes.

~~~

Cain watched her sleep. She looked so innocent lying there. He watched her for twenty minutes before he went in search of Thomas. Cain wasn't kidding when he said he wasn't leaving. But first, he had to clear it with the man of the house.

"She's sleeping now. I…she told me she wouldn't take anything for pain. I think she'll heal quicker if she has some good rest, but I understand now why she won't. I'd like to be able to stay with her, if you don't mind, that is."

Thomas was sitting in an easy chair in the spacious living room. The room, like the man, was warm and comfortable. The furnishings were old, mostly antiques, Cain was sure. The room had a wonderful lemony smell like beeswax and honey.

"Of course you can stay. I'm not particularly fond of you sleeping together, but I understand things are a bit different from when I was a young man."

Cain didn't say anything. He hoped Alyssa would allow him to stay with her even if they didn't make love. Just holding her right now would be enough.

"I'm glad she told you. Her mother laced her drink with Benzodiazepine, enough to knock a grown man on his butt. Too much for a small seventeen-year-old girl, it's a wonder they didn't kill her. I had the vomit analyzed just after Rodney got her shirt to me. It terrified me, I'll tell you. I even went so far as to have her father's death looked into. But he died of the heart attack, they said."

Cain nodded. He also understood the bottled water now too, and her strange ritual of opening one. She would squeeze the bottle and then shake it vigorously. He'd seen her do this several times in the hospital. Now he knew that she was looking for leaks, either caused by pin holes or a broken seal. He wondered if her need to check the bottles still had her doing it while she was here and he saw the five cases of water in the corner near the door.

"She told me that she has two brothers. Do you know where...what am I asking? Of course you know where they are," Cain said with humor. "Do you think they have been involved in her recent issues? Or her uncle?"

"No, I don't believe so. Robert is much too lazy to do anything that requires him to move off the couch. Nathan, her oldest brother, has been in and out of rehab for years. Small wonder his brain hasn't been cooked with all the crap he puts in his body. But he was a very nice young boy. Nathan is Samuel's son."

Cain nodded again. Christ, her family was really fucked up. Cain sat in the big chair closest to the fireplace. It wasn't cold enough for a fire, but there was one burning low in the grate, just taking the evening chill off.

The room they were in wasn't large. In fact, Cain would have guessed it to be about half the size of the smallest bedroom in the house he'd just bought. The furniture while old, was well cared for and maintained.

"She is confronting her mother and uncle on Friday morning," Thomas said, almost seemingly talking to himself. "I know she'll do fine, but I tell you, I worry. Her mother is not going down without a fight. She has no idea that Alyssa is back; that's why she's staying here. Her family had been spending money like it's theirs to take. Drew is looking into what that is going to entail and how Alyssa can make them pay it all back."

This was a surprise to Cain. He knew that Alyssa had a plan and had an idea it had something to do with her family, but he didn't know her mother didn't know Alyssa had finally been found. The two men talked for a bit longer and then Cain went up to bed.

He took his bag with him this time; the medical one was already in Alyssa's room, but he now took his overnight case. He didn't want to upset her, but did want to make it clear to her he wasn't leaving. Unpacking a few things, including his personal pack, he stripped down and crawled into bed with her. When she curled over onto him, Cain felt like the king of the world.

Alyssa was wealthy, he knew this. He'd talked to Devin and Damon in the hospital about her and was surprised by just how rich she actually was. It wasn't just the money, though that was a tremendous amount, but her holdings alone were enough to stagger a man.

He hoped that he could convince her that he loved her before she figured out their differences. Cain didn't think that Alyssa was either a snob or one of those who thought that if one wasn't a blue blood than he or she was not worth her time. No, what worried him were his mother and father. If she didn't give him a chance because of them, then he really couldn't blame her at all.

~*CHAPTER TWENTY*~

Alyssa woke to the shower running in her bathroom. Her mind was still fuzzy so she couldn't think how she had managed to turn the shower on and go back to bed. When she rolled over and felt the pain, she remembered Cain being with her and what he'd said about staying. Her eyes popped open wide.

It took a few minutes to find her robe and she flushed when she thought of the fact that she was naked beneath it. She thought about him undressing her and then washing her hair, and she wasn't sure if she wanted to be mad at him for it or to feel something else. What that would be, she wasn't sure. She made her way to the bathroom, trying her best to hold onto the anger. It would get her, though, she knew.

The bathroom door was open and steam billowed out of the room, fogging up the bath and the area just outside. She went to the large shower, her shower, and knocked hard on the glass. She couldn't see Cain for all the fog, but she could make out an outline of him.

"Morning, love. How did you sleep? I slept like the dead," he told her through the door.

"Don't you 'morning' me, you arrogant ass. I told you to go home. I'm fine and I want you to...I want you to..."

All thought flew out of her head when he opened the door and stepped to the opening. The water was still streaming down behind him and it washed over his body in long rivers. Her mouth was both dry and watering for him.

She'd seen him before, a few days ago, as a matter of fact, but this version of him, the wet and hard one, made her ache with need. His hair was dark now from the water and hung down to his shoulders in a slightly wavy mess. His face was covered in fine whiskers that darkened his chin and jaw and gave him a very bad boy look. Cain's shoulders were wide and thick, making her think of pads football players wore. His nipples were peaked and extended and she wanted to lean in and lick the water away and then nibble on him. His flat belly was rippled in muscles, tight from his belly to his groin. And seeing his groin made her groan.

His cock was straining from his body. It was thick and the dark head was purple with blood, engorged so much that it looked painful. When she heard Cain groan, she looked back up at his face.

"You keep looking at me like that and I'm going to be late to work. Come here, Alyssa. I want to kiss you."

She took a step back, suddenly not so sure of what she was doing there. He looked so…powerful, so manly. She glanced down at his cock again and it looked thicker to her. She swallowed twice.

"You look…do you hurt?" She felt stupid the moment she asked. Of course it didn't hurt. It was hard, but hurt? Alyssa she looked back into his face and shifted on her feet when he just stared at her.

"No help for it, I guess." And before she knew what he was going to do, he reached out and pulled her into the shower, robe and all. "I'm going to be late."

Cain's mouth slammed across hers quickly, taking her breath away. Before she could protest or even think of something to say, he had her robe off her and he was pulling her against his body. Then it didn't matter. Nothing did but him touching her, holding her, and taking her.

Cain's mouth was hot, and it seemed to get hotter the more he kissed her. His body pressed her back against the shower stall, his cock lay against her belly. Moving her hand down his ribs and to his abdomen, she brushed her fingers along the crest of his cock and felt him shudder beneath her touch. She liked the feeling it gave her to touch him, and his reaction made her want to do more, touch more of him. Moving her hand to cup his plum-colored tip, Cain surged against her hand quick.

"Touch me, Alyssa. Wrap your hand around me, baby. Feel my cock with your hand."

When he cupped his hand over hers, moving her up and down him, he rocked against her with every stroke. When he took a small step back and watched her hand, she wrapped her other hand around him and followed the same pattern. Soon Cain was leaning against the shower wall and watching her beneath hooded eyes.

It wasn't enough. She wanted more, more of him and what she was doing to him. Dropping to her knees in front of him, she licked the tip of his cock and heard him growl at her. Encouraged, she wrapped her mouth over his cock and swirled her tongue over him. He pressed her closer to him by curling his hand to the back of her head even as he started to fuck her mouth.

At first, she let him fuck her this way, his cock filling her mouth and her tongue tasting him. As soon as she moved to another position, moving to the side to slide her tongue along the length of him, she was rewarded with his hissed "yes." Sliding her hand up his thigh, she gently cupped his balls in her hand and rolled them between her fingers, feeling their weight. Taking one into her mouth, she thought he was going to smother her as he pulled her so close to his body.

Cain pulled her head back and she nearly cried out when he did. The sudden loss of him made her whimper. It took her a few seconds to realize he was speaking.

"I want to come in your mouth, Alyssa. I want to feel you swallow my cum. But if you don't want to, now would be a good time to stop. You've got me so close I'm going to come before too much—Christ, woman."

Taking him back into her mouth, Alyssa worked harder. She wanted to feel his cum as it filled her mouth. What she lacked in experience, she made up for in wanting to please him.

"Touch yourself for me. I want to watch you fuck your hot pussy while you suck me off. That's it, baby, play with your clit."

Moving her free hand down her belly, she paused when she found her navel. It had always been sensitive, but now it was like touching a live wire. Cain's groan could have meant he wanted her to move or to continue, she didn't know or care. Now, right now, it was about pleasure, his and hers.

Alyssa had never touched herself in a sexual way before. She had done so when she'd been in the bath, but nothing to make her feel the way she did when her fingers came in contact with her hard nub. When she slid a finger into her, she moaned and nearly pulled away from Cain's cock. His hand at the back of her head again held her in place.

"Baby, Christ, you feel good. I'm going to...I'm coming!"

The first splash of his cum hit the back of her throat and she nearly gagged, but a quick swallow and she needed more of his spice. Lifting her hand from her pussy, she cupped his balls again and rolled them. Then she moved behind him to his ass. Even as he rocked into her mouth, the muscles in his ass tightened and rolled. Before she could explore more of him, he was pulling her up his body and dropping before her as she had done him.

His tongue speared her clit. She had been concentrating so hard on his pleasure, she hadn't realized how close or how needy she'd become. When Cain slid his fingers up into her and nipped at her again, she came apart. Her body surged hard over and over against his mouth. And just when she thought she was coming down, he'd bring her back to another peak, tossing her over the edge with his mouth and fingers. She couldn't take any more, her knees weak with it. He stood up and pulled her into his arms. His cock was hard again and she looked up at him.

"I don't know if I will ever get enough of you. I can't finish what we've started. I didn't think to bring protection in here with me. I will next time. The thought of taking you in the shower...Christ woman, the things I want to do to you, with you."

He held her for several more moments, and then he helped her wash her hair again. When he turned her around to gently scrub her back, she could feel his cock as it brushed against her. Moving back against him, she felt him press hard then pull away. She laughed at him.

"Behave. Your back still hurt?" he asked, then growled at her. "I can't be late...well, anymore late than I already am going to be. I still have to go by the house and pick up some fresh clothes."

"I'm sorry. I don't know that...you probably have things you need to do. I'll just go out—"

"Don't, Alyssa. That isn't what I meant. I want you. I want you more than I've ever wanted anything in my life." He reached over her and turned off the water once they were rinsed. "We need to talk. But tonight. I have to see to Quinn and Jazzie, then I want to come over and talk to you. Will you be here?"

"Yes." She was suddenly shy and wasn't sure now as to what she should do. Cain seemed to know and handed her a towel. "I have to stay here for a few more days. I can't...I need to be here at least until Friday."

After she wrapped herself in the white fluffy cotton, she went into the bedroom and started to make up the bed as he finished up in the bathroom. She was right about the whiskers, she thought; they were dark against his skin. She was just finishing up dressing when he came out.

"Where do you work? You said you were new to the area. I didn't...I guess I didn't realize you already found a job," she asked him when he seemed to be just standing there.

"I've lived here a few months now. I work with...I'm partners with Damon Grant in his private practice. This is my first week. What are...I don't know what you do."

She didn't either, but knew that's not what he meant. Alyssa had to regain control of her family business, toss her mother and the rest of the family out on their ear, and try to make sense of ten years of financial records with her personal accounts and her business. She had to relearn all the companies and what they were worth to her and how she could help them. Then there was learning to be a person again, being around people, talking and interacting with staff, friends, and business associates. Nothing really, she thought, depressed.

"I have a few things to do around here. Thomas and I have a game of chess we're working on. I...what happens now, Cain?" Alyssa flushed. Leave it to her to be blunt and right to the point. He grinned at her and then stalked toward her. There was no other way to describe how he moved, like liquid sex.

"What happens now is that we get to know one another. I want to be with you, be a part of your life and you a part of mine. But tonight, we'll talk tonight. All right?"

She nodded. They could talk. But she wasn't sure about being a part of his life. She didn't know how to be a part of anyone's life right now. And wasn't sure she wanted to even if she knew how.

After he left, she went to find Thomas. He had told her that Drew was coming over today and after yesterday, she wanted to see if that was still true. She thought maybe she'd fired them both a number of times and wondered if either of them would still speak to her, much less work for her.

~~~

Cain managed to be only five minutes early. And though it was technically early, he still felt as though he was running behind. Of course it didn't help that every time he stopped for more than, say, two minutes, his mind wandered to Alyssa and what she might be doing right then. It was noon before he found the time to call his house. Jazzie answered on the first ring.

After he found out how she was feeling and if she'd heard from Quinn, she launched into her plans. Plans from Jazzie could be scary or insane, depending on how much effort she put into them.

"I've been trying to figure out a job to keep me busy. I know that I said I'd wait for a few weeks, but after all this, I'm bored. Know anyone who might be hiring a slightly used up jack of all trades?"

"No. But I'll keep an ear out. Have you heard from Mother? I wondered if she...if she called about his funeral." Cain wondered when the last time was he'd called his father anything but "him" or "he." There were other names, names not so flattering, but he wasn't going to think about those right now. Not with his funeral only days away, he guessed.

"Yes. She called my cell this morning and left a message. She wanted your number again. I haven't called her back. Do you think she has the money for his funeral and stuff? The last I'd heard, he only had about twenty bucks and that was because Mother had borrowed it from me and gave it to him."

Cain didn't want her to have his phone number. It was bad enough that she knew where he lived. Then he felt bad for that thought. She was his mother, after all. He supposed he'd end up paying for his father's services and as soon as she found out he was footing the bill, she would go all out for it, costing him much more than his father deserved. "I'll give her a call. When are you going in to see Quinn? I have rounds with Damon in an hour and thought I'd stop in and see her then. When I spoke to her earlier, she said the doctor hadn't been in to see her yet."

"I just talked to her. Did you know that Alyssa called her? I guess they talked for a long time. Quinn said that Alyssa was very sweet to her, but avoided talking about you every time she mentioned you. Did you piss her off again? Cain, I really want her as my sister. You'd better fix this."

Cain laughed at her tone. Jazzie could be very protective when she wanted to and she was extremely protective of what she considered hers. Cain was the same way. Especially when it related to his family, and now Alyssa. "No. I didn't get a chance to talk to her much last night. She and I are going to talk tonight. Will you be all right there by yourself another night? I don't...I'm not sure what Alyssa's plans are right now."

"Why don't you bring her back here? I'll make dinner and then you two can 'talk' all you want. I won't bother you at all." Cain grinned at her tone when she said the word "talk," as if she didn't believe they'd be doing much of that.

He hoped not either, but knew that they did have to talk eventually. He told Jazzie he'd have to call Alyssa and let her know. The other line was ringing and he told her he'd talk to her later and hung up. He wished as soon as he realized who it was that he'd had someone take a message.

"Hello, Mother. What can I do for you? I'm kind of busy."

"Your father is dead, I would think the very least you could have done was call me and told me how sorry you were about it. That damned policewoman just shot him in cold blood. I'm going to sue."

Cain took several deep breaths before he trusted himself to speak. He knew that she'd just lost her husband, but wondered if she even thought about what he'd done to his own daughter or what he'd planned to do if the money had not come when he'd demanded it.

"The police had no choice, Mother. He was going to kill someone and had been warned, several times I might add, to drop his weapon and to step back. He advanced instead of stopping, leaving the 'damned policewoman' no choice but to kill him. You do know that he was planning to kill Quinn if he didn't get the money, don't you?"

"So you're going to side with the others instead of defending your own dad? I should have guessed that's what you'd do. I suppose that money-grubbing whore was a part of this too. You know if you're going to give away your money to strumpets, you might as well just give it to me. I need it now more than any of you do anyway. You're young enough to start over, but I'm all alone."

Cain marveled at his mother. She had managed to turn his father into a saintly man, ignore the fact that said father planned to kill his own daughter, call Alyssa a whore, and a money-grubbing one at that, and demand his money all in the same breath. Unbelievable.

"Mother,'" he started as calmly as he could. "As of this very moment, I want you out of my life. Never do I want to hear from you again. I don't want you to come around me, call me, or even think about me. I've had enough. I'll make arrangements to pay a part of your husband's funeral bill, but nothing more after that. I've never been so sick of or ashamed of anyone in my entire...Don't call here again. The staff will have instructions to not put your calls through. And for your information, that 'whore' is going to be my wife if she'll have me."

Cain had the satisfaction of slamming down the phone as she was still talking. He didn't know what she was saying and frankly, didn't care. Sitting back in his chair, he thought he felt good, really good for the first time in months, no, maybe years. Leaning forward again, he picked up the phone and called Alyssa.

~CHAPTER TWENTY-ONE~

Alyssa stared at the two men in the office with her. She couldn't figure out how they could suck all the air out of the room and still be able to breathe. She looked longingly at the window to the left of her. She could honestly say that she'd give just about anything right now to be inside the big box she'd lived in for all those years. But there was nothing she could do about it now. Sitting up straighter in her chair again, she cleared her throat. It didn't seem to matter to the men, they continued on with the argument that they'd been having for the past hour. Her shrill whistle shut them up.

"As I was saying…Christ, you two are driving me insane. There isn't any way that she is going to go quietly in the night. I want my mother to sign off on the house and whatever else she took from Daddy. Monday at the latest. I have paid for enough of her stupidity." The phone ringing at her elbow had her scream.

Lucky for the caller, Thomas answered it and not her, not that she would anyway. That was something she wasn't really keen about doing just yet. She looked over at Drew. He was going to be a great asset to her if she could ever get him to loosen up. He was by and far the most uptight man she'd ever met.

"Tomorrow, I want you to look into that project for me. I just want you to look for now. There is the building on

Tenth Avenue that will suit better. And for the love a Zeus, will you please bend a little? I've seen telephone poles with more flexibility than you."

"All right. There is also the matter of household staff. Are we still going to conduct interviews tomorrow? I can run background checks on most of them from the hotel, but extensive ones will take a little longer."

She needed someone she could trust in the house. Not just trust, but someone she could get along with too. Drew had set up three different hotel rooms over the city to conduct one on one interviews for everything from cooks to yard help. No one would know who they were interviewing for and wouldn't unless they were called back for a second interview. She thought it was a sound ideal.

"Do what it takes. I also want you to find Lily for me. Find out what you can about her and do a check on her too. She is aware that you're coming to see her. She said that she'd meet you in the warehouse on Hudson Avenue on Thursday morning."

"Miss, the phone is for you. It's Dr. Waite. Shall Drew and I leave the room for you? I have things I, too, would like to add to the list of potential questions for the hired help."

Her entire body felt sweaty all of a sudden. No one had called her in…well, never since she'd been back. She eyed the phone with the feelings of terror and trepidation. She nodded to the two men and picked it up.

"Hello, sweetheart. How's your day going so far?"

How did she answer that? Did he care or was he calling for…she stopped that train of thought. It wasn't going to get her anywhere.

"I'm trying to find people to work for me when I go home on Friday and staff for my office both there and at home. I'm terrified out of my mind that the board won't accept me back. Not that they couldn't, but I don't like not being able to get along with them. I have three pro…no, four projects that are making me insane. I miss my daddy more than I thought I ever would. My mother is spending my money to pay me rent in my house. I need to pee really bad, my head hurts, and I want to go outside and run through the trees on the back lot until no one can find me. I have to take the driver's test on Tuesday and I've never driven a car in my life." She brushed away the tear on her cheek. "How's your day so far?"

He was quiet for so long that she nearly hung up. She'd scared him or repulsed him. Either way, he was going to tell her that he wasn't coming over tonight and more than anything she'd been doing today, that was the one thing that had kept her focused. And she wasn't even sure why.

"Quinn can run an office better than anyone I know. I can ask her to help you out until you get someone else. She's been looking for something anyway and this will help her out. Jazzie can organize things for you at home. I know she can run a kitchen. She ran a five star restaurant until she got bored and quit one day. I have my driver's license and a car. I could teach you how to drive in a couple of afternoons. I'm sure if you just got up and went to the bathroom, everything on your desk will be there when you return. The mom thing…can't help you there. Sounds like you need a good attorney. Take two pain relievers for the head and take a break in the woods, if that's what you want. I'm sure you'll feel better. Did I miss anything?"

Alyssa burst into tears. Not just tears, but sobbing her heart out, nose running down her chin, hic-uppy tears. She could hear Cain talking to her, but she couldn't answer. In less than two minutes, he'd fixed it all for her. Thomas came into the room with his cell phone to his ear.

"Yes sir, I can see her now…yes, she's crying very hard. What did you say to her? I will hurt you if…oh, I see…ah, yes…no, I don't see that it will matter one hell of beans to…oh what a splendid idea. I believe she is calming now, sir. Shall I tell her to talk to you now?"

Thomas handed her a box of tissues and shook them in front of her. Putting down the phone, she took several out and blew her nose. Next, he handed her the trash can. She glared at him as he stood there. After depositing the used tissue, she started to pick up the phone again when he cleared his throat. He was holding the antibacterial stuff in his hand, ready to squirt it into her palm. She was going to murder him in his sleep.

"May I pick up the phone now, or did you want to disinfect my shirt too. I'm sure there are…oh, I don't know, maybe several billion germs on my feet as well. Want maybe I should dip them in that crap too?"

"Don't be crude. I would like you to stay healthy. Now talk to that young man. I have errands to run. I'm also picking up that disgusting pizza you wanted for lunch. Would there be anything else?"

"No. Not that I can think—yes! That movie you told me about. Can you see if you can find it too? Pretty please with sugar on top?" She batted her lashes at Thomas and could hear Cain laughing as she put the phone to her ear.

"You would do well to learn to beg like that more readily, I think. As for the movie, I have already purchased it. It is in the living room. Also, just so you know, cook has been making all your favorites tonight. Will Dr. Waite be joining you for dinner?"

Before she could ask, Cain answered. "Tell him yes, if that's okay with you. What am I having anyway?"

Alyssa nodded to Thomas and he left the room. "I don't have a clue. I have been eating whatever they set in front of me for a week now. It's easier than arguing. I'm going to be as big as this house before I leave." She leaned back in her chair. "Thank you. It was just suddenly too much."

"I wish I could help more. You actually helped me too. My mother called. I'll talk to you about it tonight. You really should just take a walk. I wish I could join you. I love the outdoors too."

They talked for a few more minutes and when they hung up, she went to the bathroom and took two Ibuprofens. Going into the kitchen, she sat in the chair and watched Mike cook. He didn't say much even when he was deep in conversation with someone, and she liked that about him.

"Mr. Thomas said you got a man coming over for dinner tonight." He set a glass of iced tea in front of her and some cheese and crackers. She only shook her head. Not for the first time since she'd been staying here did she wonder where they kept all this snack food that they could just pop it down in front of her whenever she sat for more than two seconds.

"Yes. Dr. Waite. Did you meet him?" She knew that Cain had been here, but didn't know how much of the staff he'd met.

"Yes, ma'am."

She sat and watched him, not really paying any attention, her mind off on the things that she had to get finished before Friday, plus, she was about to cry again. She thought of Jazzie.

"Mike, there's this girl I'd like you to meet. Her name is Jazzie Waite. She's Dr. Waite's sister. Cain said she ran a restaurant some…what?"

He was staring at her with a surprised look on his face. And a silly grin. She didn't know what to make of either.

"Miss Jasmine Waite? I know of her, yes, ma'am. Her name is legendary with the Chicago food trade. I heard she took on three head cooks out in the Marquis LeBlanc 'fore she decided on a newcomer. That restaurant is so booked up 'cause of him that they have people waiting for months to get a table."

Alyssa stared at Mike. That was the longest conversation she'd ever heard him utter since she'd been here. Then she realized what he was saying. "Jazzie is famous? Great! Cain said she'd come and cook for me if I asked. Or at least run my kitchen. You think I should hire her?"

"I think if you didn't, I'd have to hurt you myself. She can do it, run your house too, I'm betting."

Alyssa decided to call Cain back and tell him that she'd take Jazzie on. Then she thought of the other women in his life. Pulling out the cell phone that she had only just gotten this morning, she called his office again. "Hi. I was wondering if you'd invite your sisters to dinner tonight. I know that Quinn gets to come home, right?"

"Yes. Jazzie has just gone to get her. I think they were going to stop by anyway. Quinn wanted to talk to you about something. Would you like for them to keep you company until I get there? I should be out of here at about five."

"I haven't asked Mike yet if there will be enough food." She grinned when he didn't even turn around, but nodded at her. "Yes, that'll be great. If you could let them know to park in the back, I'll see them then."

~~~

Cain watched his sisters as they sat around talking at the big table. Thomas had joined them, as had Mike. Mike was in awe of Jazzie and had barely said three words all evening. Thomas told them stories of when Alyssa was a child and had everyone laughing at some of the stunts she'd pulled.

"She was such a precocious child. Her father would have given her the world had she but asked him. Of course she did not. She worked for everything he gave her, including his company."

Alyssa looked uncomfortable and he decided to change the subject. He asked about her driving lessons. He thought she looked like a lost child sitting there and he wondered about it.

"Her father had purchased her a car for her birthday. Her sixteenth, I believe. He was so happy to have found her one. It is a Shelby Cobra, a nineteen sixty-six, I believe. The two of them restored it that entire summer." Thomas smiled at the memory.

"You had a muscle car" Cain asked her suddenly 'Holy shit! Really? I've only seen them in pictures. What color was it? I'm betting fire engine red with red and white seats. Wow!"

"It wasn't red, it was blue. Dark blue with white leather interior. Daddy wanted to paint it red, but I'd read this article on how red cars get tickets quicker than…what?"

"Blue? There should be a law against girls picking out the color for cars," Cain said.

He was on a roll now. She was actually looking better now than she had all evening. Maybe he needed to keep her mad at him to keep her feeling better. Nah, he thought, sexually aroused was much better.

"I like blue. Was it fun to drive, Alyssa? I'm betting you even followed the speed limit, too. Cain would have had thirty tickets before he'd left the street if he had one," Jazzie huffed at him.

"Thirty? Hell, I would have been lucky to have made it to the end of the driveway without getting arrested. What happened to the car, Thomas?"

"It's in the garage at the mansion, sir. I've had it under lock and key since the young miss went…now what?"

Cain was on his knees before Thomas could finish. He wasn't above begging for a chance to touch the car much less the opportunity to drive it. He would have to pay through the nose if he was caught…if he was caught. "You have to tell me that it's still drivable. Please, Thomas, don't make me have to beg. I will be your slave for life." Alyssa's laughter had him turn to her. "You have no idea what this car can mean for all mankind, love. It's like the super sexy model of cars. Men would do and have done very scary things to own this car."

"And yet it sits in my garage. What do you think, Quinn? What should we make him do to drive such a car? I'm thinking take us to the spa and sit with us all day. What do you think?"

"Only if he had a pedicure as well. I think then maybe you can let him sit in it. For an hour."

Cain looked at his sisters. They were laughing. He'd thought once before that they didn't laugh enough. And both times he'd realized they were laughing it was because of Alyssa being with them. He turned back to Alyssa.

"I can make you pay, you know. I have…ways to make you scream for mercy."

Her blush made his cock twitch. He wanted her right then. She seemed to realize that as well. Thomas speaking broke the spell, but not the thought of taking her upstairs and ravishing her body.

"I can have the car tuned up tomorrow. No one will think anything of it. I will make sure that it is safe to drive as well. The insurance is up to date, so that is no problem. Is that all right, miss?"

"Yes, Thomas, that's perfect. Thank you. Could you also warn the State Police on Monday that Cain will be driving it and if there are any fast moving blue UFO's flying low to the ground it's probably only him?"

Thomas looked down at Cain, who winked at him. The look on the older man's face was priceless. It was a combination of confusion and seriousness. Cain burst out laughing. "Ah, Thomas, it's going to be a blast getting to know you. I think I'll like having you around."

Cain and Alyssa went outside to walk around the back of the property just after dusk. The weather was nice for mid-May and the wildflowers were just beginning to break through the ground.

"Thanks for having the girls over. I think they had a great time. I know I loved it." He reached for her hand and was glad that she didn't pull away from him.

"I like your sisters." They walked a little more before she spoke again. "What did your mother want today when she called? Jazzie said that she had called her as well."

"To tell me that my father's funeral was going to be expensive and that she didn't know how she was going to pay for it. I told her that I would pay reasonable and customary. Nothing more. Did Jaz seem upset about it?"

"No, just resigned. She told me that your sister Sin was overseas and wouldn't be home for the funeral. I'm sorry for that. But she said that the other two would be here in a few days. Quinn said that Gracie Anne was coming to be sure he was dead."

Cain smiled. That sounded like her. Gracie Anne could tear a man to sheds when she thought they needed it. A woman too. Cain thought that she and Alyssa would get along fine.

They walked along a little more and now that the house was out of sight, Cain stopped them. He'd been thinking about Alyssa all day and wanted to taste her in the worst kind of way. Turning her in his arms, he pulled her to his body and pressed his cock into her softness. "I've been hard most of the day thinking about you. I'm glad I had a long lab coat on or I would have terrified most of my new staff and patients. You taking me into your mouth...Christ, I want you."

"Twice today I had to go to the bathroom and cool off my face. I thought that I'd die of embarrassment every time Thomas asked me what was wrong. I wanted to go down to your office and jump your bones, Dr. Waite."

Cain covered her mouth with his. She tasted of the chocolate cake she'd had after dinner, sweet and dark. When her arms wrapped around his neck, he reached down, cupped her ass, and lifted her. Her long legs wrapped around him and she hooked her ankles at his lower back.

Without taking his mouth from hers, he palmed her left breast even as his left hand worked at the buttons on her blouse. They were not cooperating and just when he was about to rip it from her, she slapped his hands away and did it herself.

"You are so impatient. Were you planning to tear the buttons off? What would I have worn into the house? Ever think of that?"

"I can't think right now beyond sucking on your nipple. And I could care less if you were always naked. It would save me a great deal of frustration if you were."

When she opened the tiny clasp on her bra, her breast spilled out into his hands. Warm and soft, her breasts tightened under his gaze, her nipples puckered tight, and the hard nub seemed to beg for his mouth. Lifting up the heavy flesh, he took the tip into his mouth and nipped at it. Alyssa's legs tightened around him and she rode his denim-covered cock.

"Please tell me you have a condom. If you don't, I'm going to seriously hurt you then leave you here to bleed to death."

He did, but was tempted to tell her no. But at that moment, she started working on his buttons and the sight of her small hands on him made thinking nearly impossible. When Alyssa leaned forward and took his nipple into her mouth and nipped him, he nearly came right then. As it was, he couldn't stand much longer.

"I want to taste you. I want to lick your pussy until you come then I want to fuck you hard against this tree."

Cain felt her body shudder against his and he helped her put her legs back on the ground. Sinking to the ground before her, he slowly lifted her skirt up and kissed the area as he exposed it.

Her skin was hot and each inch he got closer to her pussy, her legs trembled just a little more. Running his hand up behind her to her ass, his hand filled with her naked flesh and he looked up at her surprised.

"I took them off in the bathroom before we came out. I wasn't brave enough to not wear them all night, but I thought, had hoped, we'd be having sex once we got out here. By the way, I have condoms with me if you don't."

"Oh darlin', we aren't going to have sex." Her crestfallen face had him hurry on. "I'm going to make love to you. Right after I drink from this luscious pussy." Cain watched her as he lifted her skirt up, slowly folding it up and exposing her dark curls for him. They were wet; dewy moisture clung to the tight curls and it was everything he could do not to throw her to the ground and take her hard and fast.

Watching her, he slid his finger up to her opening and slowly moved into her heat. When she opened her legs wider for him, he moved between her thighs and kissed her there, moving his tongue along the seam and then worrying the little nubbin that was peeking out from between her nether lips. Fucking her with his fingers, Cain moved in and out of her heat, widening his fingers, scissoring them to stretch her for him. When she started to ride his hand, he used his free hand to cup her ass again, running his fingers along the seam and then along her tight rosebud.

"Don't come yet, love. I want to drink my fill of this nectar you're feeding me. You're so hot, so delicious for me. Hold on, baby, don't come yet."

His mouth began working her in earnest. She tasted like ambrosia to him. The more that he took from her, the more cream she made. His cock ached, it needed a release. The only release it wanted was the woman in front of him. Lifting his head just enough to speak to her, Cain nearly came when he saw what she was doing.

Her breasts filled her hands; her nipples tight and rosy were being pinched between her fingers and her head was thrown back in wild abandonment. Her voice, heavy and dark and filled with passion, moaned and begged him to finish her, to give her the relief she so desperately needed.

"Come. Come now," he commanded.

Her body didn't just come, it detonated. Alyssa exploded in his mouth with so much of her spice that Cain felt it drip down his chin and onto his neck. Her cries were long and loud, ripping from her throat. Even as she peaked again and then again, Cain fucked her with his fingers and tongue. When he touched the tight pucker at her ass and slid his finger into her, she screamed again, over and over until he knew she'd be hoarse tomorrow. Standing up, he jerked his fly open and rolled his condom on in seconds. Lifting her up, he impaled her on his cock as he covered her mouth again. Pressing her against the tree, Cain pounded into her. Hard, fast, deep, he took her until he felt the tingle run up his lower back and grip his cock. Just as he shot his cum into her, he slammed his finger deep into her ass again and brought her with him, tossing them both over the edge into paradise.

~CHAPTER TWENTY-TWO~

"My father had been an abusive man all his life. And my mother idolized him for whatever reason. It wasn't until I was nearly an adult before I realized that she was more in love with him than she was with being our mother."

They had come back into house twenty minutes later and his sisters were both gone. Thomas said he was going up to bed and told them good night. They were sitting on the couch with a low fire burning in the grate.

Alyssa loved this room. It was warm and inviting and the furniture was soft and worn. There were two couches in a V in front of the large fireplace. A large, round coffee table took up most of the area between them. The walls on either side of it were enclosed bookshelves that held more than just books, but items as well. Things that his children had made and things their children had made as well. She was staring at a picture of Thomas and Drew at his graduation when she thought of her dad and Thomas.

Her dad had told her that when Thomas' wife had passed away, he wouldn't let go of anything that had been hers. Even after all these years, Alyssa was sure her clothing still hung in their closet and her things still about their bedroom.

"Your mother is a piece of work, but then so is mine. How many times…I'm sorry this isn't any of my business. How are your sisters taking—"

"Don't. I want you to know about them. How many times what? Finish, please. I want you to ask. I'm beyond being embarrassed about them anymore."

She didn't think that was quite true, but she asked anyway. "How many times had your father been in jail? I mean, from what I heard that night in the warehouse, it seemed like a lot."

"Six times before I graduated from high school then when I was in my first year of med school, he went to prison for murder. He'd been drunk and impatient sitting at a light. The guy in front of him didn't move fast enough for him so my father drove around him and up onto the sidewalk. There was a family just coming out of a shop and he ran them all down. The man died at the scene and the woman, his wife, was expecting their first child. She lost the baby and then later committed suicide."

"Oh, Cain, I'm so sorry. That must have been horrible for you and your sisters. And that poor woman, to lose so much."

Alyssa curled up in his lap and held him to her. He didn't say anything for a long time. He just held her and ran his fingers up and down her back, careful even though he'd taken her hard against the tree not an hour ago.

"No one has ever thought about how it affected us. My father spent ten years in prison and as far as I know, none of us ever went to see him. He'd call me a few times, Quinn too, but we never talked to him much. My mother would try to get us to visit him. But again, none of us would. He was an abusive man. He hit them and me until I started fighting back. If he was to catch one of the girls alone, he'd knock them around a bit, but never Sin. Sin would have kicked his fucking ass. In fact, I think she did once or twice."

"I think I'll like Sin. Where does she live? And the others, where do they live? Close by?"

Cain laughed. "Sin is in the Special Services. She's overseas right now. She can't tell us where, but I hear from her about once a month. Her real name is Sydney, Sydney Valeria. She and Lilliane Iris, or Lilly-pad for short, are identical twins. But you couldn't meet two women more opposite. Lilly-pad has a lot of fire, but she is a kindergarten teacher. I suppose she'd have to be tough to do that too."

"Teachers need more than our support, I think. I think they should be canonized. Large statues should be erected for them. I'm going to try and set up a fund for the local schools when I get back to work." She actually had a whole list of projects that she was going to take care of when she got back to work. Several of them were already in motion and a couple more were still being worked on with details. Closing her eyes, she took several deep breaths to calm herself.

"Whatever you're thinking, it'll be fine. Your mother can't hurt you unless you let her. I know. I have the same problems."

"Tell me about the rest of your family, please. You said you have five sisters. I've met Quinn and Jazzie, both of whom I love by the way, and then Sin and Lilly. Who's the last one?"

His voice was a soothing balm over her nerves. Being in his arms was like being held in a warm blanket on a chilled night, watching the fireflies flitter across the sky. Alyssa started to ask him something else when she realized that she was in love with him. Sitting up, she looked down at him. Cain gave her a questioning look.

He was so handsome and kind. She loved the way he made her feel. The things he did for her and to her. She was in love with him.

"What is it, baby? Are you all right? I wondered if I had hurt you out there. That was stupid on my part. I should have—"

"I love you."

~~~

Cain couldn't breathe. She loved him. Alyssa Howard loved him. He pulled her back down so that her forehead rested on his and he held her. "I love you too. I never...I've been such an ass." She burst out laughing. "No, let me start again. I've been an ass to you so many times over the past few days. I've wanted to tell you at least five hundred times in the past...I love you, Alyssa. With all my heart, I love you."

She lay back down on his chest. He didn't know what to say to her now, not that he couldn't think of about ten thousand things to say, just nothing came to mind. He wanted to hold her love secret but also shout it to the world. He wanted to call Damon and tell him, the man who'd been more a father to him than his own had been. But he also wanted to savor it just a little while longer. When she spoke again, he grinned.

"I've never been in...I've loved people before, but never been in love with anyone before. I loved Rodney, but I wasn't in love with him. My daddy, I guess, but not like I love you. He would have liked you. No, that's not true, he would have loved you. He always told me that he would need to approve of the man I brought into his family. Not that I'm saying we need to get married. I don't want to, I've got..." She sat up and looked at him again. "He would have approved."

Cain wasn't sure what to think about her not wanting to get married. He would do it tomorrow if she would say yes. Of course, he should probably ask her first, but he didn't think right now was the time. He could tell that she was stressed and last night when they'd gone to bed, she'd tossed and turned quite a bit before he'd pulled her to him and held her. She had muttered about her mother and her uncle for some time. When she started to tell him about them, he wasn't surprised. It was a heavy weight on her mind.

"I know I told you about my...I'm going to do something on Friday to her. Something that only Thomas and Drew know about. I'm going to kick her out of my house, her and my uncle. And then I'm going to cut her off. I have the right to do so and according to my daddy's will, I should have done it long ago. I've been...she'll hate me more than she does now when I do it. But I can't let her continue on as she's been doing. She'll run the company into the ground if I let her. You understand, don't you, Cain?"

The fact that her mother was hurting Alyssa was enough for Cain to want to agree with her. But he knew that's not what she wanted or even needed. She needed assurances, not someone to blindly agree with her.

"You mother won't change, will she? You don't believe she will suddenly become mother of the year and want you and her to have the kind of relationship that other mother/daughters have? If you did, then you would give her another chance, right?"

"Yes. She would hurt me now just as quickly as she did before just for the money. And you know what? If I thought it would make a difference to her, I'd give it to her. But she'd just find something else to turn on me with. Daddy left a video will just for her, he said. He said he wanted her to see his face when he told her she was a...let me think. Oh yeah, 'a lying, two-timing fucking bitch with no morals and no sense of pride.' Dad had a way with words."

Cain started to laugh, hard. He was sure that he knew that because Nathan's daughter was much the same way. And Cain thought that Nathan would have been very proud of her.

They went up to bed a little while later. Cain held Alyssa until she fell asleep. He wanted to start on a life with her as soon as possible and wondered if she'd want a large wedding or would she be happy with just a simple one? He thought that a woman of her stature would need to have a big wedding and decided he didn't care. As long as she said "yes," he didn't care if they got married in a bar in the lower East side as long as she was his.

Cain decided that on Friday, he was going to propose. She would be finished with this thing with her mom and hopefully ready to move on. He was going to go to the jewelry store tomorrow and wondered if he should take his sisters. Then he decided against it. He wanted to do this on his own. Closing his eyes, Cain went to sleep with a smile on his face.

~CHAPTER TWENTY-THREE~

It was Thursday afternoon and everything was going according to plan. Drew sat at the desk opposite from Alyssa and watched as she went over the last contract that they had drawn up. It was a standard agreement, much like the ten others she'd signed in the past six hours, but she still read every line. And he loved it.

He looked over at the files on the chair they still had to go over. He was sure she'd want them finished before Cain came home. She was nothing else if not a perfectionist. Nathan Howard had left his billions in the right hands. Alyssa was going to triple the company's net worth in ten years or Andrew Miller would eat his hat.

"Okay, I guess I can live with this one too. I don't like that they won't let us tear the company apart for thirty days, but I can see their reasoning. But we both know that there is no way they are going to be able to keep it afloat."

This company she was buying simply for the building. It was a downtown high-rise that had been converted into a bunch of shops from top to bottom. It might have worked except there was nowhere to park to shop at them. Alyssa had bought the building with the stipulation that she gave them thirty days to try and reorganize, then they could buy the building back. He told her it was a sound idea in that it wouldn't work and she couldn't do anything with it until the city gave her the permits. That took about the same amount of time.

"Okay," Drew said as he handed her two more files. "There are these two things that cannot wait. The first one is the clinic. I have the building purchased for that and a line on the medical supplies it will need to run. I also have a list of doctors who have agreed to help you out by donating one day a month of their time. The name has been registered and will be unveiled when the building is emptied."

"The Rodney Kincaid Clinic is something I'm going to be very involved in. I want you to set up whatever they need when they need it. Thanks for rushing this for me. It will help a great many people."

He nodded. Grandda had told him a little about Alyssa's story, but not all. Drew was sure there was more to the clinic than either one of them had said. But the fact that the place was going to be named for a fallen policeman was enough to get him on board. He handed her the two things that he needed her approval on.

"The city is asking that you don't let the homeless clutter the sidewalks outside the building and that you make sure that you have sufficient guard when you're open. I explained that we'd be open twenty-four/seven and they aren't happy with that either."

"Hummm, well fuck them. I purchased the block, right?" Drew nodded even as he smiled. "Then the only business that I'll be cluttering up is my own. If they call again about this tell the current mayor that I'm planning to run against him if he gives me anymore shit. I have lots more money and I know how to use it. Next."

Drew handed her the next file as the phone rang. He could tell by her face that it was Cain. He'd never seen two people more in love. He started to rise and she waved him back down.

Drew knew that she wasn't going to like the next file. It was about the mansion and the issues he'd run into since he'd started his "remove the fucking bitch" job. He glanced down at the file tab and smiled at what she'd dubbed the file. RTFB/job. He laughed every time he read it. Drew liked working with this woman.

"Okay, I'll see you tonight then…I love you too…all right." She hung up with the sappiest grin on her face he'd ever seen.

"Want a minute? Your cheeks are bright red. I'm sure I can go and find you a freezer to step into if you want."

"Fuck you. Now what else? And just so you know, I don't want you to save the worst for last anymore. I know you do it. Put it somewhere in the middle, or better yet, the first thing. I would prefer to end on a semi if not good note when we do this in the future, okay?"

"Sure. But this had to wait until the end. I want it to be the first thing you think of in the morning when you confront her."

She paled slightly and sat back in her chair. Drew couldn't imagine having to do this to his mother. She would have skinned him alive if he'd even tried. But over the past several days, he came to realize that Alyssa's mother was nothing like a normal mother, not even close. She was a money hungry bitch and knew no boundaries when it came to getting what she wanted.

"All right, give it to me. Oh! Before I forget, did you find anything on Lily? I do want to have that information when she comes in on Monday."

"Yes, I did, and you're stalling. Lily's paperwork is on this desk somewhere. You are paying for your brother Nathan's rehab and Robert's alimony. Both of which are costing over seven grand a month each."

"Pay for the rehab for another six months then stop. He finds a job and I'll help, otherwise he's on his own. Does

Robert have children?" Drew shook his head no, thank goodness. "Then stop that as well now. I'm not paying for a failed marriage that everyone had to know wouldn't work from the beginning. Uncle Samuel?"

"He was just diagnosed with testicular cancer six weeks ago. His chances of having a child are slim to none unless he had sperm saved before he started chemo. I've contacted his doctors and his specialist, and they are both aware that Howard monies will not be footing the bills for any more of his treatments that are experimental." Drew looked up at Alyssa when she snorted. "I agree that drinking a bottle of eight hundred dollar wine is a bit excessive and I told the doctor that too."

"And he said what? That he will try something with an eight dollar bottle? I'm not paying for that either. Okay, now Mother. What is she up to?"

Drew handed her several sheets of paper. He hoped that she'd agree with what he'd proposed to her. This was going to be tricky even with what he'd done.

"About you mother...she's spent over three million dollars this year already, not including the money you're paying her rent and utilities with. She seems to think that you are her own personal bank account. I've...Alyssa, I've taken steps to recoup some of your losses. On Friday after your mother and uncle leave the house, a team will come in and ransack the place in that they will be looking for anything and everything on that list. The locks will be changed and the staff let go. When the recovery team is finished, a salvage company will come in with an accountant to see what else there is—clothing, shoes, and anything personal that can be sold. Everything else will be boxed up and put into storage until such time as I can see what its value is."

"All right. I don't like it, but I agree that it has to be done. I want you to do the same with my brothers' and my

Uncle Samuel's places too. There is no telling what is there."

Drew made a note to get another crew lined up for that. "I have a cleaning crew to come in and get the house ready for you. Your things here will be packed up and taken to your house and the new staff we've hired will start Friday evening. The gardens have been neglected as well and I have a staff coming to get those in order as soon as possible. Those won't be repaired over night, but by the end of summer, you'll see an improvement."

She looked resigned and tired. He had been working with her for five days straight for ten or twelve hours a day and he knew that she was working long after he'd left and before he arrived every day. He closed the file up, knowing there were a few more things to clarify and okay before too long, but he knew she needed a break. After putting the file in his briefcase, he stood up.

"I have a date tonight. I'm sorry but you'll have to finish these up on Friday or Monday at the latest. Can you think of anything that we really need to close tonight?" Drew knew that her mind was going a hundred miles an hour, but she wouldn't keep him from his plans. He was going to love working with her; she was going to be a great boss.

"No. Nothing that...you're going to be there tomorrow, aren't you? I don't...I don't want to get myself in a place where she can get what I've worked so hard to take care of."

"Yes. I'll be there. If for nothing else then for the entertainment. It's going to be quite a show. I actually can't wait."

Drew wanted to take her into his arms, but she didn't seem the type to be hugged. He'd seen her reaction to Grandda hugging her. It was as if she didn't know how to do it or she had forgotten. Drew thought that Cain would be good for her. He liked to hug and to touch her, his sisters too.

He left a little after four and decided to call Cain on his way home.

~~~

Alyssa sat on the ground in front of the headstone. She brushed away a few twigs as she thought about tomorrow. It was going to depressing, pathetic, horrific, and exciting. None of which she was looking forward to. She looked at the headstone again as she spoke. "You'd like Cain, Daddy. He's a good man. I'll bring him by to meet you soon." There was laughter just over from her and she watched two children run around while a man sat on a chair next to a headstone similar to the one she was at.

"Tomorrow I'm going to toss mother out on her ass. Sorry, her butt. She...her and Uncle Samuel have been up to no good and I have to do this. I'm sure you would have approved." She traced the letters before her. The dates hurt her so much. He would have been sixty this year, she thought idly, and turned to lay on the damp ground, her head where his heart would have been. She let the tears fall as she continued. "I failed you, didn't I? I should have...I should have stayed and faced her, faced them, but I was a coward and a wimp. I was so hurt that you'd left me and I just wanted a minute to be...she wouldn't let me mourn you. I miss you so much, Daddy. I'm so sorry."

She lay there for another hour, her heart hurting and her tears falling. She rolled to her back and looked up at the tree that shaded where she lay. Her dad would have loved this spot.

"I'm going to go now. I have so much to do tomorrow, but I'll be back. I want you to meet some friends of mine, some of them new and others I've...they helped me." Sitting up, she leaned over, kissed his name, and sat back down. "Do me a favor and find Rodney for me and tell him that I love him too. He was a great man and he loves to play chess. Find him and play a game for me."

She walked back to the car and slipped inside. There was no one with her other than the driver and she closed the window between them and wiped her tears. Tomorrow she'd have it all back and she would do everything she and her daddy had talked about and more. She was going to make it up to him, make up to her daddy when she'd left.

When Alyssa got back to Thomas' house, she went to her room and took a long bath. She had called Cain earlier and asked him not to come by, that she was too stressed out and wouldn't be much company tonight. She wanted him there, but wasn't sure what he would think about the things she would be doing in the morning. She was just stepping out of the tub and wrapping a towel around her when the door opened.

"I thought…what are you doing here? I was going to go to bed early and then…what are you doing here, Cain?"

"I got us a movie to watch. And Thomas is making popcorn, extra butter for you and natural for him and me. I also picked up one of those Danish you like, cheesy and full of fruit." He took off his tie and tossed it on the counter. Then he toed off his shoes and unbuttoned his shirt. He was taking off his cuff links when she stopped him.

"What are you doing? Put those back on. You're…you need to leave here right now. I've made plans that—"

"Break them." His voice was husky and full of heat. It was all she could do not to strip him down and take him on the floor. "I'm going to get into the tub with you. I want to make sure you're very relaxed and sated before we head downstairs." She watched, mesmerized, as the shirt pooled on the tile floor and he took off his belt.

"I don't want to…" Her mouth was dry and no matter how many times she licked her lips, they just wouldn't be satisfied. "You should go, Cain. I'm not going to be fit company tonight. I've got things I need to—"

"So do I. I have lots of things I need too. Like for instance, this towel. I would like it so much better over there on the rack, don't you think?"

He pulled it away from her body and tossed it in the general direction of the hanger. Cain pulled her closer to his body, but he didn't let her press against him. She could feel his heat, his warmth coming from him.

"Cain, you were supposed to...stop that. You should be at home and...and..." He was touching her, no, not touching really. He was skimming his fingers along her skin and making her body crave more.

When his mouth touched the place where her neck met her shoulder, she thought she'd melt into the floor. His breath was like a warm blanket spreading over her. Alyssa could feel his fingers touching deeper, his hands moving over her more and his touch more defined.

"Alyssa, do you still want me to leave you?" His body moved against her now, pressing fully to her and heating her more.

"Cain, please. Please, don't...no, please don't leave me."

Suddenly, she was lifted up and into his arms. Before she could protest or even make a sound, his mouth was covering hers. He moved them both out of the bathroom and into the bedroom without pausing. He laid her on the bed and stepped back. She wanted to cover herself, and even lifted her hands to do so when she looked into his eyes.

Lust. Passion. Need. Love. Each emotion slipped over the other until she couldn't tell one from the other. He only stared down at her, not moving to remove anymore clothes or to join her in the bed.

"I wanted to tell you again that I love you. I've never…I didn't think it would ever happen for me. With you it's…perfect. Everything about you is perfect."

Tears welled in her eyes. She knew she was nothing close to being perfect. But from him, his words, she felt it. She reached for him and he leaned down to her. When he covered her with his body, she rocked up into him. Alyssa could feel his cloth-covered cock press hard against her soft folds.

"Cain, please. I want you inside of me. Deep and hard. Take me, please?"

He rolled to his back and worked at the button and zipper at his pants. Alyssa sat up to help and found herself straddled over his thighs with her knees bent into the mattress. When they had his pants open and his boxers pulled down enough for his cock to be free, she scooted back on his legs and leaned down to take him into her mouth. He stopped her with his hand to her hair.

"No, honey, this is about you. I want to please you."

Reaching behind her and to his fingers in her hair, Alyssa pulled them from her head. She brought his hand to her mouth and licked then suckled each finger. When she pulled his index finger to her mouth, she groaned. His answering groan raced along her skin.

"Alyssa, you're playing with fire right now. I want to give you a night of pleasure, but if you keep that up, I'm not going to be able to."

Popping his digit out of her mouth, she grinned at him. "But this is pleasurable for me. I want your cock in my mouth, Cain. Will you let me taste you again? I want to feel your cum as it slides down the back of my throat."

~CHAPTER TWENTY-FOUR~

Cain watched her as she leaned down again. Her eyes were on his as she licked her lips then ran her tongue along the length of him. He was going to die, he decided. Right now his heart was so erratic that he was sure that if tested, they would declare him in d-fib. When she got to the swollen head of his cock, Alyssa wrapped her tongue around him then took him into her. Before he could think about how hard he did it, he surged up into her heat.

"Alyssa, baby. Please, take me. I want to—Christ!"

She wrapped her mouth around him and swallowed. Her throat tightened around him, milked him. Cain wove his fingers into her hair and held her to him. He was close to coming, his cock felt tight and painful. When Alyssa cupped his balls, she let his cock go from her mouth. But before he could protest, she lapped at him and made her way down. He could feel his balls ready to release, the sensation racing along his spine and down the length of him.

"Come for me, Cain. Let me have you. Let me taste all of you."

Her breathless command was all he needed. He could no more stop the eruption from shooting from him even with a gun to his head. With a roar, he came. Over and over, his body let go, filling her with his essences until he couldn't move—until he didn't want to move ever again.

As she made her way up his body, nipping and kissing him as she went, Cain felt his cock stir. By the time she was at his nipples, he began to feel a tightening in his groin, his cock come alive. Rolling Alyssa to her back when she bit his neck, he felt as though he could conquer the world and needed her now.

Covering her mouth with his, Cain reached into the side table drawer and pulled out a condom. He was glad it was that easy. Had he needed to get up and find his pants he would have taken her without protection. Then the uninhibited thought of her belly swollen with his child filled his mind.

He looked down into her eyes as he sat up and rolled the condom onto his hard shaft. Her body was ready, hot and wet; her curls were glistening with her cream. He was sure that he'd never seen a more beautiful sight in all of his life.

"I love you, Alyssa. With every cell in my body, I love you. There has never been anyone before you, I realize now, and there will never be anyone again. You are my life, my heart, and my soul. I love you." He entered her slowly, stretching her, filling her with not only himself, but his love. When he was fully seated within her, he looked at her again and marveled that she could be his. Before he could say anything more to her, she spoke.

"I love you too. I...oh, Cain... I love you more than I thought could be possible. I want to spend the rest of my life with you, be happy with you, make a home with you."

Cain began to move in her, slowly pulling out and then moving just as slowly in. He wanted this to last, this miracle of finding her, knowing her. Kissing her, tasting her mouth, the wonderful taste that was wholly her, he moved deeper still, took more and gave more. As his peak grew closer, he could feel her body building with him, pulling and milking him. Just as she tumbled over the edge, a gentle fall this time, he went with her, savoring the feel of completion and love. Knowing that for the rest of his days, this one night would be burned in his memory for all time.

Rolling to his back, Cain took Alyssa with him, her body spread over his in a limp blanket of sated woman. Reaching for and finding the blankets, he pulled them up and over them. Cain reached for his phone, and saw that it was much later than he'd thought. At just after midnight, Cain set his alarm, snuggled down deeper into the bed and closed his eyes with a happy smile on his face.

At ten after three, his phone rang. For several seconds, he didn't have a clue where he was. When he pulled his phone to his ear, Alyssa pressed her bare bottom up to his groin and it was all he could do not to groan in the phone.

"Dr. Waite, we have a patient in the emergency room of yours. Miss Danielson said that you've only seen her twice. Would you like us to call the on-call physician or would you like the ER doctor to treat?"

After getting some of the details as he stood up, he told the nurse that he'd be in. He didn't want to start out on the wrong foot with his care to those he saw, and he grabbed his pants. He was reaching for his shoes when Alyssa woke up.

"Everything all right? It's not your sisters, is it?" She looked so good laying there he wanted to join her.

"No, a patient from the office. She's complaining of chest pains and has a history of chronic angina. I'll be back when I can. Will you be here?" He had spoken to Drew at length this afternoon about Alyssa. He knew that tomorrow...today she had a meeting with her mother. Drew told him that it wasn't going to go well and that she would probably take whatever happened between them very hard. Cain also knew a little more about Alyssa's background with her mother too.

"No...I'm going to go to a meeting at the Howard Building sometime in the morning. I don't know when I'll be back from it. Then I have to see to several…can I call you later? I won't if you have to stay focused on your patient."

"You call. If I can't answer then leave me a message and I'll call you back. If it's an emergency, call the hospital. I'll leave word that if you call me to put it through. I have the same thing with the girls." Cain leaned down and kissed her. "I love you. Call me, okay?"

She nodded. He wasn't sure, but he thought there were tears in her eyes, but she turned over onto her belly and he was no longer sure. Slipping out of the house, Cain quietly went to the front door and left. Thomas had given him the code yesterday and he didn't have to worry about waking the house.

Cain was waiting on the blood work to come back when he went into Miss Danielson's room. She was an elderly lady and he liked her a great deal. She'd told him in the office that she'd never been married and regretted that some. He was surprised to learn that she was in her late nineties. Sitting in the room's only chair, he held her hand when she reached for it.

"I'm old, not stupid. Now tell me what you know about this old heart." He grinned. She was also very straightforward and told him she liked her news that way too.

"Yes, you're old, but not quite ready to bite the big one yet. I think you've got a little lung infection and it's causing you some discomfort." Her snort made him raise a brow.

"Discomfort? Sounds like I bumped my big toe and you want to put a band aid on it. Tell me, damn it. Am I needing to go into the nursing home or not? Got my daughter in one of them things, can't stand it. She poops herself, if you can believe it. Seventy-five years old and she can't even make it to the pot. I don't want that to happen to me."

"You don't need that route if you keep taking care of yourself the way you are. You have a healthy heart for your age and you are still of sound mind. I would like to suggest that you find someone to come in and see to your needs once or twice a week, more if you enjoy it."

She smacked his arm. "You married yet?" He shook his head no. "You should be. Nice young man like you. There a woman or a man in your life then?"

"There is a woman, but she's a little…we aren't exactly on the same side of the railroad tracks. She's more of an uptown rich girl that drinks mimosas for lunch. Me? I'm more of a beer-watching football sort of man."

"Huh. Maybe she likes a beer on the couch with a man screaming at others in tight pants. Stupid reason not to get with her, don't you think?"

Cain supposed when one put it like that, it was sort of a stupid reason. He still didn't know what to do about Alyssa. He did love her. Very much as a matter of fact.

"I'm ninety-seven years old, Doc. Never been married. Had the chance too, but thought he was too good for me. Turned out he was perfect. But I was too slow and he died when I was in my thirties raising a little girl he never did see. Now I mourn a man who I have a child by 'cause I was too stupid to see reason. You going to be in that same boat? Mourning a girl that you don't have? Or you planning to marry one you think more suited to you?"

Cain didn't say anything. She was right. He had been planning to walk away when this…whatever it was ran its course. He didn't want it to end, but he knew…he thought he knew how it would end. "I don't have any plans that far in ad…we are talking about your health, Miss Danielson, not my personal life. You really should have a—"

"Hush up and listen to me. My name is Sadie Sue. Now I don't expect you to name your first born after me, but it'd be nice. I want you to stop fussing with me. Hell boy, I'm old enough to be your great, great, great grandmother. Now, you leave me here to stew a bit and then tomorrow, I'll go home and get me one of them live-in nurses. I want you to go and get that girl a ring and you go straight to her and you get down on your knee and propose to her. What she going to say? No? So what then? You know. But if she's smart and I know she is if you love her as much as I can see you do, she'll say yes. Then you bring her here to me so I can get a proper hug for putting you two together."

Cain couldn't help it he started to laugh. He didn't realized how much he needed it until he'd started. He squeezed her hand once again and stood up. He really did like this old woman a great deal and knew that Alyssa would as well. "And if I do and she says yes, you going to dance with me at our wedding? It'll be a big affair. My sisters want it to be in the gardens. You okay with that?"

"You get her to say yes and I'll do a jig at your wedding. Now get out of here and I don't want to see you for at least a day or two. I mean it, boy. You do right by her and she'll make you the happiest man in this earth."

Cain leaned down and kissed Sadie Sue on the weathered cheek. "She already has. Thank you. I'll hold you to your promise."

He left the hospital an hour later. It was nearly nine o'clock in the morning and he was tired. But more than that, he had a plan. Getting in his car, he called Damon and got some names of jewelers. He was in the showroom of a friend of his twenty minutes later.

~~~

The meeting was just being called to order when Shannon stood to address the room. No one seemed to know why the meeting had been called, or they weren't telling her. But Shannon was going to make it known that as acting president, she would not tolerate someone doing this again. She had only planned to spend half a day here today and this was cutting into her time with Carlos, her newest lover.

The thought of what that man could do with his tongue and fingers had her shiver with anticipation. He had brought her to peak four times this morning and she didn't want her relaxed aftermath fucked up by some upstart who thought she shouldn't be in charge. Well, she'd show them, by God.

"I would like to know which one of you idiots called this meeting. I've told you before if you want to be in charge, you can try and take this company from me." She looked at each person at the table straight in the eye. They wouldn't look at her long before turning away. She knew how to intimidate people better than anyone she knew. It was all in the breeding, she thought. Just her being better than them financially made her more superior to them.

"Good then. I'm leaving. And the next time—"

The doors to the conference room behind her opened and she turned, ready to blast whoever dared to interrupt her. She was in charge and the sooner they got that through their fucking heads, the less she'd have to fire them. Cows, stupid cows, it was all they were.

When Thomas walked in as if he owned the place, Shannon was ready to snarl at him, put him in his place once and for all. Why he was even allowed in the building anymore was beyond her and was something she was going to take care of as soon as she put him in his place.

"Forgive me gentlemen, ladies. Mrs. Howard. But we were running a little behind. Just one more...ah, here we are."

Before Shannon could say a word, Thomas stepped out then back in again followed this time by a woman, a very beautiful woman. Shannon could only stare.

"Hello, Mother."

"Oh my...Christ! It's you. You're...you're...Alyssa?"

"Yes. So nice of you to remember. Everyone, please be seated. I shall be with you momentarily."

Shannon only just realized that everyone had stood when her daughter walked in the door. Shannon looked around the room suspiciously. She thought they knew. None of them seemed the least bit surprised to see Alyssa there. Shannon wasn't sure what to do. Then she noticed the man standing directly behind Alyssa.

Alyssa moved to where she was standing and Shannon thought her daughter was going to hit her. Alyssa looked so...so grown up that Shannon was sure she would never have recognized her if not for that dark hair, so much like her father's. But there was something else about her too, something hard and unforgiving, cold even. Shannon thought she should try and hug her daughter to show the board and Alyssa that she was a good mother. When she reached out to touch Alyssa, she stepped back so quickly that she backed into the man behind her.

"Don't touch me," Alyssa snarled at her. "Don't you ever touch me again."

Shannon was mortified. Rebuked by her own child, her own flesh and blood, and in front of everyone too. Before she could admonish her for her rude treatment, Alyssa spoke.

"I believe you're in the wrong room, Mother. This meeting was to between the president of Howard Enterprise and the members of the board. As you are neither, I want you to leave. Now."

The voice, it was like hearing Nathan all over. The cold and calculating way he said things. The way his voice became hard and unbending. Shannon nearly looked for him in the room.

"But Alyssa, I've been...you've been...I've been running this company for ten years and I won't be—"

"Oh but you will, Mrs. Howard. You will leave now or security will help you out. Your things are already with them. Would you please come with me?"

210

Shannon looked at the young man beside Alyssa now. "Just who the hell do you think you are talking to me like that? I'm Shannon Howard and I will be treated with more respect or I'll…"

"You'll what?" Alyssa asked with a bit of a hard laugh. "There is nothing you can do. Perhaps you'd like to meet my attorney, Andrew Miller. Andrew has been very…well, I guess so have you. Been very busy, I mean." Alyssa sat in the chair one the board member, Shannon didn't have a clue which one, had pulled out for her. "I wouldn't fuck with me today, Mother. I'm not a child any longer and I'm not going to forgive and forget. Drew," Alyssa said as she turned to him, "if you would be so kind and to take out…take out the trash, I would very much appreciate it."

Shannon looked at the board members. She hoped that at least one of them would come to her aide. A daughter just didn't treat her mother—the door opened again and four armed security guards stood there. One held a box and even from a distance, Shannon could see it was full of the things from her office. The office she'd just had decorated again. Anger burned through her.

"How dare you have these…these people." She pointed to the guards. "How dare you have them go through my personal things? You've no right to do that."

Alyssa stood up, her grip hard on the table. Shannon could see her knuckles turn white. When Alyssa simply nodded to the men, the guards as one moved toward Shannon. She turned once again to her daughter.

"Alyssa, you can't do this to me. You can't humiliate me like this. I'm your mother. I've…I've missed you." Shannon hated to beg, but there was just too much at stake here and she needed to backtrack quickly.

"Goodbye, Mother." As Shannon was nearing the door, Alyssa called out to her again. Shannon nearly fell over in her haste to turn. Finally, she thought, finally Alyssa was seeing reason.

"You've been moved out of my house on Lincoln, as well as the other houses I own. I've had you set up in a nice house on Diaz Lane. The accounts have all been changed and you no longer have unlimited funds. You might want to consider that before each purchase for a while. The monies that you've spent…well, I'll let Drew talk to you about them at a later date. There is a credit card with a limited amount of money on it you can spend according to the terms of Daddy's will." Alyssa nodded again and Shannon was out into the hallway.

The door closed behind her and before she took two steps away, loud applause resounded from the conference room. Shannon was escorted to the service elevator. She looked at the guard next to her.

"This is all a misunderstanding—a mother/daughter spat. You'll see. You should just let me have my things back in my office and tomorrow we'll all laugh about this." At least Shannon sincerely hoped they would.

The guard turned to her and smiled. Shannon took a step back. This was not a friendly smile. No, this one was more of a snarl than a smile. Then he spoke, his voice was just as frightening as his smile.

"You make one move without my say so, Mrs. Howard, and I will take great pleasure in blowing a hole in your heartless chest. You may not remember me, but I do you. Three days after the young miss in there disappeared, you fired me and then told my new wife that we'd slept together. All I can say is it's a good thing she's a loving woman and didn't believe a single word that spewed from your mouth. You go on thinking it's a spat and I'll be waiting for you to try and make Miss Alyssa see it your way." He took the box from the other guard and shoved it into Shannon's arms.

"You have a nice day, bitch." As the elevator doors closed tight, it left her standing in front of the Howard building.

Shannon found herself on the street, quite literally. When one of the guards came outside and toward her with a smile, a nice one this time, on his face, she thought for sure they were all realizing the mistake. When he reached out, she actually held out the box in her hands, thinking he was going to take it back upstairs for her. But he simply reached out and jerked the name badge off her blouse, tearing a small hole in it. Stunned, she turned to look at the man speaking to her as the guard with her badge walked back into the building.

"...said to take you to your new home. She done paid me already so let's get a move on. Meter's running."

The man, a cab driver, took her box of things, put them in the trunk, and then got back into the taxi. He didn't even hold the door open for her or take her hand as she was led inside. Why, she'd never been in a taxi in her entire life. Shannon just stood there. The back widow opening startled her. Samuel stuck his head out of the back window.

"Damned girl threw you out too? She's gonna have to pay for this, Shannie. I don't think she should be treating her own kin like this." Samuel slid over. "Get in, we need to talk. And doing it outside the enemy fortress as it were isn't such a good idea."

If Alyssa was back, she now controlled the money again. Shannon didn't like that. She had plans, expensive plans. She looked at the driver. "I want you to take me to my house on Lincoln. I have things—"

"Sorry, lady, I'm to take you to Diaz Lane and nowhere else. You want to go somewhere else after that then it's up to you. I got my orders."

They sped down the road and Shannon just knew that things were going to, if they hadn't already, hit the fan. She used a phrase her late husband used all the time. It seemed appropriate right now.

"Fuck a duck and watch it waddle. We're so screwed."

~*CHAPTER TWENTY-FIVE*~

It was nearly noon when she asked them to take a break. Alyssa had been running on pure terror since her mother walked out...had been escorted out of the room nearly two hours ago. Lunch was being catered and Mr. James, one of the board members, was telling her all the things she shouldn't be doing with the Kincaid Clinic.

"Mr. James. As I have said several times now, the clinic is a nonnegotiable item on the list. If you bring it up again, I will have to have you removed from this room. That being said, if you have any more objections to this project, put them in writing and send them to me. I will give each reason careful consideration. But the clinic stays."

"Your father would have been—"

"My father trusted me. I won't be browbeaten every time I spend my money. This board was put together as a courtesy to those of you who wanted a piece of the action. You are in no way associated with Howard Enterprises and as such, have no real vote here. I am giving you the details of what actions I am going to take, again as a courtesy. If you don't like what I'm doing then I'll buy you out. I'm sure that Andrew will help you out. I would like to..."

The door had opened and she looked up in time to see Cain standing there. He smiled at her and crooked his finger at her to come to him. She stood up and was moving toward the door when Drew cleared his throat and smiled.

"You want to adjourn the meeting first there, boss lady?"

"You want me to kick your nuts for you there, law boy?" She looked at his face. "You knew he was coming here?"

"Yes. I thought you could use someone in your corner, or maybe a kissy face time out later. He's been here since eleven. Cain probably needs some time with you too."

Alyssa looked at the man sitting there. Drew was all right and she liked working with him. She told everyone that they would be meeting again in one hour and then leaned down to Drew. "There's a fat raise involved if you buy out Alex James before the end of next week. A substantial one too."

"How much?" he whispered back. "Worth me putting an offer on that new car I want 'substantial?'"

"Worth you buying the car and the boat too 'substantial.' Friday, noon, and I will make it six figures. Deal?"

He jumped up so fast he tipped the chair back onto the floor. She was still laughing when she went into the hall. Cain took her hand and led her down the hall. He steered her into her daddy's office. The door was clicking closed when he had her pressed against the wall and his mouth over hers.

"I've missed you."

Cain leaned his head on her forehead and looked down at her. They were both breathing hard and she moved against him.

"I missed you too. How's your patient? Is she all right?"

He looked at her and smiled. She'd never seen that particular smile on him before and it sent chills down her body. It wasn't a bad smile. On the contrary, it was very nice.

"I love you, Alyssa. Very much. And the fact that you asked about my patient…she told me to come here and speak to you. Her name is Sadie Sue Danielson. We don't have to name our first born after her, but she wants us to think about."

Alyssa put her hand on her belly. Did he know something she didn't? Was she pregnant even now? She suddenly felt weak in the knees and started to slide to the floor.

"Hold on, sweetheart. You're fine. Let me explain." She wanted him to, but then again, she didn't. Then he grinned again. "Can you stand up on your own yet?"

"Cain, tell me what you know. I'm so…am I pregnant? I forgot to get the…what are you laughing about, you hyena? This isn't funny." Cain dropped to one knee and looked up at her. She didn't know what to think and could only stare down at him. "Cain?"

"Alyssa Howard, I love you with all my heart and I would very much like it…no, I would very much love it if you'd marry me." The little ring box suddenly appeared in his hand. She stared at it with an open mouth. Then she looked at him.

"If I'm pregnant, then you don't have to marry me. We can—"

"I have no idea if you're pregnant or not. I love you and I want to marry you. However, in the very near future, like immediately following you saying yes, if you want to work on said baby then I'm okay with that too." He wiggled his brows at her. She, of course, started to laugh.

"You really want to marry me? Seriously? And have a baby with me?"

"Very seriously. And I want to have lots of babies with you. I want to spend the rest of my life with you." He shifted on his knees. "Honey, this floor is hard and my knees aren't.

Can you please say yes so I can stand up and kiss you properly?"

She continued to stare down at him. "Marry you? Why then? I mean…" Cain watched as she made her way to the large desk and sat in one of the chairs facing it. "You'd have to put up with me. I'm not…I don't do well around people."

Cain felt himself relax. This had nothing to do with him not being in her class of peers, but more to do with her insecurities. That, he felt he could deal with. He stood and walked to the desk, but instead of sitting in the chair beside her, he sat in the chair at the desk.

It was covered with files, though they were all neatly arranged. There were pens and pencils in a holder and a ruler with highlighters in a tray next to it. A state of the art laptop sat open; the screen saver "Howard Enterprises" danced across it. A book, a manual really, was open and several sticky notes hung from pages. The title Computers for Dummies made him remember how much she had missed in the past ten years.

"This desk, it was your father's? He used it?" Alyssa nodded. "And he left it every night cleared of project and memos, no matter how late he worked?" Again, she nodded.

"Being married to me would be a second place position, Cain. You'd have to be the person behind all of this." She waved her hands at the desk. "I don't have…I don't know how to leave things until later." Cain thought that was untrue, but left it for now.

"My father would be here last in the evening and in well before anyone else came in the next day. This was his life's work. It will be mine as well. Marrying me would be a mistake. We should just live together."

Cain leaned back in the big chair and regarded her. She looked so lost, so forlorn that he wanted to gather her into his arms, but knew that this was important to them both.

"Did you spend time with him here, Alyssa? Or was he here alone every night?" He nearly smiled when she bristled.

"I know what you're getting at. Well, you're wrong. He didn't stay here to get away from me. We worked hard together, he and I. He loved me. We built this company together."

"Of course he loved you. That isn't what I was saying at all. But who is the one person he didn't spend time with when he was here? You think that's who he stayed here to get away from?"

He could tell by her face that she hadn't. He watched as she processed the time she spent with her father and who he hadn't spent time with. And why. Cain let her as he looked around the room.

The desk was massive. He thought it was at least six feet long and as much as three feet wide. The design on the top was beautiful with its different types of light and dark woods inlayed into it. The front facing him was a long column of drawers two by two on both sides of him. There were tall shelves along the walls. Most of them were filled with books, but a great many had frames and art as well. The dark walls were offset by the wall to wall floor to ceiling windows that let in the bright sunlight. Cain looked back at Alyssa when she spoke.

"My mother isn't a nice person. She hates me. She'd hate you just to spite me. Or she would try to recruit you into turning against me."

"That isn't going to happen, baby. I love you. And I know all about hateful mothers. Remember mine? She is as mean and nasty as they come." She nodded then looked at him. "Will you marry me, Alyssa Howard?"

"I have a business to run just as you do. I want that clear right up front. I don't want to hear how I'm neglecting you."

Cain stood up. She was saying yes and he wanted to be close to her when she realized it.

"Yes. I have patients that need me as well, and I may have to leave in the middle of dinner and our children's dance recitals and plays. Some days, I'll be home early, others, I won't."

Alyssa turned in her chair and looked down at him when he dropped on his knees before her. She wasn't smiling yet, but he could see she was getting there. He pulled out the little blue box.

"I'm going to open a place where the people on the streets can come and get an education and a job if they want. I may even hire them for the experience. I'm going…I've opened a clinic, the Rodney Kincaid Clinic for them as well."

Cain nodded. "I'll work the kitchen lines if you need me. I'll even see if I can get others to donate their time as well." Cain pulled out the ring and put it on the tip of her finger. "Alyssa, you've stalled long enough, tell me yes."

She looked down at him and nodded. "I'll marry you. But I want you to know, I'm going to make your life a living hell most of the time."

"I wouldn't have it any other way."

Cain went to the meeting with her. There was some talk about the absence of someone named James, but he paid little attention. Cain did notice that Drew was looking at cars on his phone off and on. Alyssa stood up as soon as everyone was seated.

"Everyone, I have an announcement to make. As of ten minutes ago, I just became engaged to Dr. Cain Waite."

Drew nearly tossed his phone at her. The look of shock on his face was priceless as he looked between the two of them. When he stood up and pulled Alyssa into a hug then Cain, it was perhaps the greatest moment of his life. The rest of the people in the room seemed equally happy for them.

"You work fast, buddy. I hope you know that I expect a raise for hitching you two up. I did tell you to come here today." Drew grinned as he shook Cain's hand.

"I'll see what I can do."

~*CHAPTER TWENTY-SIX*~

Six months later

The wedding day dawned bright and beautiful. The caterer was to arrive in two hours and the tents were all up. Tables and chairs delivered the night before were being set and flowers fussed with. The wedding cake was put on the table with large bowls of fruit and chesses. The gift tables, already groaning with the weight of hundreds of gifts, were being guarded by the security guards from the Howard Building. Everything was nearly perfect. Except that the bride and groom were missing.

The house was in an uproar. Cell phones were being used to hunt them down. There was a policeman there taking notes on when they were last seen and what they were wearing. He was about to put out a state wide bulletin when Thomas came down the stairs with a note in his hand and an odd smile on his face.

"She is all right. She has taken Cain to meet her father. She assures me that they will be back in plenty of time."

"But...I thought her father was deceased. I mean, he died some time ago, didn't he?" Jazzie said from the couch.

"So he has."

~~~

"Daddy, I'd like you to meet Roscoe Cain Waite, Jr. He doesn't like the Roscoe part, so we'll leave it out from now on. Cain, this is my daddy, the greatest…one of the greatest men I knew."

Cain leaned down and put his hand on the headstone where Alyssa stood. She had tears in her eyes and he handed her his handkerchief.

She was beautiful. They were both dressed in their wedding clothes. She in her long white gown, heels, and veil, and him dressed in his black tux and cummerbund. Her flowers were lying on the ground next to them.

"Mr. Howard. It's very nice to meet you. I want you to know that I love your daughter with all my heart and will make her happy with my dying breath."

Alyssa laid her hand over his. "Daddy, Cain and I went to the pancake house this morning. We caused quite a stir when we arrived dressed like this. But everyone was so nice. Cain even ordered a plate of the blueberry ones for you to eat. Extra bacon too. Then we came here. I wanted…I wish you were here with us, with me."

Cain started to step back, to give her some time. But she pulled him to her and kissed him. Then she held him again.

"We are going to have a good life together, Cain and I, Daddy. We do love each other and trust each other. I know that I've been telling you all about the things I've been doing and how things with the business are going, but…"

She looked up at Cain and smiled. It was a watery smile, but happy, he thought. He kissed her gently on the mouth and brushed away the tears.

"Daddy can't be with us today so I…I'm glad that you didn't mind doing this with me, so that he could be a part of my day. I miss him very much."

"No, baby, I don't mind. But I made some arrangements of my own. I know that you come here a lot, to talk to him and to work things out. So I thought it would be nice if we were married here. We'll still get married at the house, but this one, this place, will be for us."

The minister came out from behind the large vault and stepped toward them, Drew and Quinn right behind him. They too were dressed in their wedding clothes.

"He's going to be right here with us, like he will be for the rest of our lives. I couldn't give you your daddy to give you away, but I can give you this."

"Oh Cain."

Alyssa tumbled into his arms and he held her as she sobbed. Everyone stood back enough to give her what she needed. When she was ready, Cain Waite married Alyssa Howard in the cemetery by a big tree with her daddy in attendance.

Before she left, she leaned down, kissed the top of the marker, and gently rubbed her hand over it. Cain heard her whisper to her father to make sure he watched out for Rodney, that she loved him too.

About the Author

Hello! My name is Kathi Barton and I'm an author. I have been married to my very best friend Sonny for at times seems several lifetimes – in a good way, honey. And together we have three wonderful children and then the ones we brought into the world - Paul and Dale Barton, Jason and Wendy Barton and Danielle and Ben Conklin. They have given us seven of the greatest treasures on Earth. They don't live at home seven days a week! No, seriously, seven grandchildren – Gavin, Spring, Ben, Trinity, Sarah, Kelly and Kian.